OF

THE DIVINE CHILD.

BY

VERY REV. DEAN A. A. LINGS,

Nibil Obstat.

REMY LAFORT,

Censor Librorum.

Imprimatur :

✠ MICHAEL AUGUSTINE,

Archbishop of New York.

New York, November 22, 1899.

Refuge of Sinners Publishing Inc.
PO Box 100 - Pekin, IN. 47165
www.MOScompany.com
1-800-451-3993

Contents

STORY OF THE DIVINE CHILD.

Necessity of a Divine Redeemer.

WE learn from Holy Scripture that many, many years ago God created heaven and earth ; that He made the fields and caused grass to grow upon the face of the earth; that He stocked the waters with fishes and the land with animals, and, lastly, that He placed on this earth an intelligent being called man.

There is then a God, an intelligent, supreme Being, infinite in power and in wisdom, who can call into existence from nothing a living being ; who knew just how He wanted this creature and for what purpose he was destined. It certainly requires an infinite power to make something out of nothing; it requires an infinite power to make a dumb animal, not to speak of a rational animal, such as man. None of these things can come into existence of themselves; from

5

nothing nothing can come. In man the development of life in nature reaches its highest perfection.

But what is this intelligent being, man, for whom the world was made ? He must be a very important being when he acquires such dominion in this world, that you might say the world belongs to him; and faith steps in and tells us that God is the origin and end of man. It teaches us the personal union of a material body and of a spiritual, free, responsible, immortal soul.

The creation of the world and of Adam and Eve is clearly narrated in sacred Scriptures, and there it is claimed that God directly created our first parents; hence we may know that all the many millions of human beings who now live in this world are descendants of that first man and first woman, Adam and Eve.

Man has a soul and a body; with the soul he knows God the Creator, loves Him and serves Him, and because that soul is immortal, can never die, he expects also always to serve God in heaven. The body is useful to the soul in giving it a habitation, in giving it the external expression of senses, in giving it an opportunity to live in society. But this body is very short-lived; very few of the human race reach a hundred years; after that they

are carried out to the graveyard, and that is their
end as far as this world is concerned. But the
soul will live on for untold centuries, for a coming
eternity; in fact will never die.

When the world had been prepared for the habitation of man almighty God also planted a garden
for him, Eden or paradise, and we believe that
garden to have been supremely beautiful; the
sun shone there always; the climate was temper-
ate; plants grew in magnificence, and animals of
the stateliest kind came there to serve man. In
our day only a few animals, such as the horse, the
cow, serve man; the others are wild and fierce, and
not only do not obey man, but threaten his life.
Adam and Eve were placed in this beautiful garden; this park so magnificent that the expensive
parks of the present day are not to be compared to
it. The whole world was probably a paradise;
everything was beautiful, was perfect. Man was
therefore relatively a perfect being of his kind.
It is inconceivable that the human mind could
have raised itself to its present heights from a low,
degraded, barbarous state. God would not create
a being of that kind and then bring it by degrees
out of the depths of misery to a higher perfection.
The first man came forth from the hands of God
perfect and in the height and fulness of life. In

His infinite love and wisdom God created man for a definite end and purpose: so that the soul is the image of God and as such must tend to God as its author.

How long man is in this world the Scriptures tell us: it is not really very long; six thousand years may look long to us, but what is that in comparison to the millions of years it took to bring the world to its present condition? And many people have lived on this earth since the creation of our first parents; millions upon millions have been born and have gone into eternity. They were once here, they received the benefit of the coming of the Redeemer, but passed away never to return.

When Adam and Eve were placed in paradise they felt all the happiness of youth, plenty, and joyousness, and their souls were filled by the consolation of God. God came from heaven and visibly walked with our first parents in paradise; God was pleased with His whole creation, but especially with man, for here were intelligent beings who could appreciate what God had created: these intelligent beings could look into the depths of the mysteries of God, could recognize the greatness and magnificence of His work in the creation of the universe. The intelligent creatures God had made were not necessary to His glory and happiness, but He in His goodness wished that others also should see His greatness and admire it.

One day almighty God placed a very slight obligation on His favorites in paradise in order to try them, to see whether they deserved still greater favors. The command which God gave our first parents was that they should not eat of the forbidden fruit, as is told in the second and third chapters of Genesis in the Old Testament:

"And the Lord God took man, and put him into the paradise of pleasure, to dress it and to keep it: And He commanded him saying: Of every tree of paradise thou shalt eat. But of the tree of knowledge of good and evil thou shalt not eat. For in what day soever thou shalt eat of it, thou shalt die the death. Now the serpent was more subtle than any of the beasts of the earth, which the Lord God had made. And He said to the woman: Why hath God commanded you, that you should not eat of every tree of paradise ? And the woman answered him saying : Of the fruit of the trees that are in paradise, we do eat: But of the fruit of the tree which is in the midst of paradise, God hath commanded us that we should not eat: and that we should not touch it, lest perhaps we die. And the serpent said to the woman: No, you shall not die the death. For God doth know that in what day soever you shall eat thereof, your eyes shall be opened: and you shall be as gods, knowing good and evil. And the woman saw that the tree was good to eat, and fair to the eyes, and delightful to behold: and she took of the fruit thereof, and did eat, and gave to her husband, who did eat. And the eyes of them both were opened: and when they perceived themselves to be naked, they sewed together fig-leaves and made themselves aprons. And when they heard the voice of the Lord God walking in paradise at the afternoon air, Adam and his wife hid themselves from the face of the Lord God, amidst the trees of paradise. And the Lord God called Adam, and said to him: Where art thou? And he said: I heard Thy voice in paradise: and I was afraid, because I was naked, and I hid my-self. And He said to him: And who hath told thee that thou wast naked, but that thou hast eaten of the tree, whereof I commanded thee that thou shouldst not eat? And Adam said: The woman, whom thou gavest me to be my com-panion, gave me of the tree, and I did eat. And the Lord God said to the woman: Why hast thou done this? And she answered: The serpent deceived me, and I did eat. And the Lord God said to the serpent: Because thou hast done this thing, thou art cursed among all cattle, and beasts of the earth: upon thy breast shalt thou go, and earth shalt thou eat all the days of thy life. I will put enmities between thee and the woman, and thy seed and her seed: she shall crush thy head, and thou shalt lie in wait for her heel. To the woman also He said: I will multiply thy sorrows, and thy conceptions: in sorrow shalt thou bring forth children, and thou shalt be under thy husband's power, and he shall have dominion over thee. And to Adam He said: Because thou hast hearkened to the voice of thy wife, and hast eaten of the tree, whereof I commanded thee, that thou shouldst not eat, cursed is the earth in thy work: with labor and toil shalt thou eat thereof all the days of thy life. Thorns and thistles shall it bring forth to thee, and thou shalt eat the herbs of the earth. In the sweat of thy face shalt thou eat bread, till thou return to the earth, out of which thou wast taken: for dust thou art, and into dust shalt thou return."

How clearly does this history show the fall of Adam and Eve from grace! They had turned their back on God and dreadfully did God punish them for it, for again we read: " Lo, Adam is become as one of us, knowing good and evil; now, therefore, lest perhaps he put forth his hand, and take also of the tree of life and eat and live forever. And the Lord God sent him out of the paradise of pleasure to till the earth from which he was taken. And He cast out Adam, and placed before the paradise of pleasure Cherubim and a flaming sword, turning every way, to keep the way of the tree of life."

The fall of Adam and Eve brought not only many misfortunes on themselves, but on all the human race which came after them. The fountain was poisoned in itself so that nothing but evil could emanate from it; the whole human race was bad in the eyes of God.

Prophetic Promises of a Redeemer.

The human race had chosen evil, and it went from bad to worse. A few years after Adam and Eve were driven from paradise, they had the terrible sorrow of seeing the first murder committed. Cain killed his brother Abel out of jealousy; more and more was the knowledge of God forsaken, the human race sank into barbaric ignorance in which cruelty, slavery, war, and robbery became of frequent occurrence. Surely the human race needed a Saviour who would reinstate them in the favor of God. In fact that was the first promise made to Adam and Eve even at the very time when punishment was meted out to them: for the Lord said to the devil: "I will put enmities between thee and the woman, and thy seed and her seed; she shall crush thy head, and thou shalt lie in wait for her heel."

Satan tempted the woman Eve, our first mother; he disguised himself in the form of a serpent, and the prophecy is addressed to him, in the form of a serpent. He triumphed not only over the woman but over the man through her. Between the woman and Satan enmity is placed by God Himself, and between his seed and her seed. From that time Adam and Eve began to hope that the day would come when they would be reinstated in the grace of God. In fact, then and there almighty God offered them pardon for the sin, at least if they believed in a future Redeemer, the Incarnate Son of God. The faith of the whole ancient world rested on the revelation expressed in those words of God. It was on this that Adam and Eve fed their hopes day by day, during their long years of penance. This was the object of the faith in which Abel offered his acceptable sacrifice of the firstlings of his flock. It was this that kept up the faith and animated the religious service and the practice of virtue of the long line of the patriarchs before the Deluge and after it. The words, "I will put enmities between thee and the woman and between thy seed and her seed," etc., mean that a child of that woman is also promised a victory over Satan. It is Mary with her Child in her arms, or Mary standing at the foot of the cross. This hope was the foundation of the whole religious life of the patriarchs; with time the image grew, and whenever the human heart made an act of faith, or offered its sorrow for sin to God in an act of worship or sacrifice, that act contained a memory of the words first spoken to Adam and Eve. Men at that time lived in the hope of the coming Redeemer.

People had become very wicked, and the few who kept the light of faith burning in their hearts must have sighed for the coming of the good God to redeem them. There had been cruel wars which had slaughtered hundreds of thousands in battle; whole nations were overturned, human sacrifices were offered; the most abject slavery was practised, the whole world was in a frightful confusion of vice: it was like a pandemonium, with all the devils of hell let loose and delighted to see their diabolical work going on so well.

But the promise of the coming Redeemer was not only made to our first parents, it was repeated and emphasized at different times after the Flood to the patriarchs. When Abraham was chosen by God to be the father of many nations as a reward for his faith, it was said: "In thee shall all the kindreds of the earth be blessed." And to him was given the sign of circumcision to show him that from his seed the Redeemer should spring: and thus a particular race and visible society of men was separated from the rest as the heirs of a special promise, and a covenant on the part of

God. These promises were repeated to Isaac and Jacob, and in case of Juda the son of Jacob was said, " the sceptre shall not be taken away from Juda nor a ruler from his thigh, till He come that is to be sent, and He shall be the expectation of nations." Then appeared Moses: he was the deliverer of the people from the bondage of Egypt: he was the lawgiver of the Jewish nation ; by a series of unexampled prodigies he was their guide and support during forty years of their pilgrimage in the desert.

In course of time even the particular family is designated from which the Redeemer should appear. Jesus is not merely to be the Son of David, He is to be the King of whom David was to be the prototype. David often spoke in his Psalms of the coming Messias.

The prophet Isaias, the evangelist of the Old Testament, speaks almost exclusively of the coming Redeemer. He describes His glory and even His ignominious death; in one place he says: " And there shall come forth a rod out of the root of Jesse, and a flower shall rise up out of his root, and the Spirit of the Lord shall rest upon Him, the spirit of wisdom and understanding, the spirit of counsel and of fortitude, the spirit of knowledge and of godliness, and He shall be filled

with the spirit of the fear of the Lord. For a
Child is born to us, and a Son is given to us, and
the government is upon His shoulders; and His
name shall be called Wonderful, Counsellor, God
the Mighty, the Father of the world to come, the
Prince of peace. He shall sit upon the throne of
David."

In the same manner other prophets also spoke,
and so through the whole Old Testament we find
the promise of the Messias, His near approach,
and the invitation to prepare for His coming. We
read in Scripture that when Herod was looking for the place of the birth of the new King of
Jerusalem in order to give the desired informa-
tion to the Magi, these words were quoted to him
from the prophet Micheas : "And thou Bethlehem Ephrata, art a little one among the thousands
of Juda ; out of thee shall He come forth unto Me
that is to be the ruler in Israel, and His going
forth is from the beginning, from the days of eternity."

And the last of the prophets of the Old Testament says : "Behold, I send My Angel and he
shall prepare the way before My face. And pres-
ently the Lord whom ye seek and the Angel of
the testament whom you desire, shall come to His
temple. Behold He cometh, saith the Lord of

hosts. From the rising of the sun, even unto the going down, My name is great among the Gentiles, and in every place there is sacrifice and there is offered to My name a clean offering, for My name is great among the Gentiles, saith the Lord of hosts."

Thus with figures and prophecies the mind of the Hebrew reader of the sacred Scriptures was continually turned towards that great fact, the coming of the Messias.

These considerations on which, my dear children, we have so imperfectly dwelt, will help us to see how very completely the work of preparation of the chosen people was conducted by almighty God Himself. I have but touched upon the various heads and will leave the rest to your future study in the Catechism, where all these things will be taught you. God has done all that was to be done for His vineyard. We may be certain, therefore, that there were hearts and souls ready to welcome Our Lord and His Church when the fulness of time came, and that their readiness was the fruit of faithfulness to God's word. These good people became in turn the teachers of the world outside of Israel, so that many nations treasured in their writings or in their sayings a hint as to the coming of One who would again make the world happy.

He that is to come must be the great God : the prophecies tell us of this: there is never a question that some mere human nature was able to undertake the salvation of man and reconcile fallen man to God. Every human soul needed that redemption, could only make atonement for itself—and not even that ; for what is man that he can satisfy God ? What was demanded was that a human being and at the same time a God should offer Himself for the expiation of human degradation. And none such could be found but in Our Lord and Saviour Jesus Christ, both God and man. The Second Person of the Blessed Trinity, full of affliction for His creatures, had offered Himself as a sacrifice: " Behold, I come," He said to the Father. It is therefore a God who is to be born in the world, but at the same time He is to be a man of the race of Adam and Eve. No other being but God Himself could make atonement to God. When the Redeemer shall then be born, we have none other to expect than God Himself, and all the angels will adore Him, saying, here on earth as they do in heaven: " Holy, holy, holy, the Lord God of armies."

This work of the redemption of man is the greatest of the works of God on this earth, greater than the creation of a universe, and we stand in mute astonishment when we think of it.

Mary the Mother of God.

ONE great preparation which God made for the coming of His Son into this world was the selection of a suitable Mother for Him : He was to be born in the flesh of the race of Adam, and of the family of David. We cannot imagine that the Mother of God could be an ordinary woman, she must have superhuman prerogatives ; God must have built her with the power of His omnipotence and made her in every way worthy of the duty of becoming the Mother of God.

Let us see what the Church, the Scriptures, and the piety of the faithful think of that great being, the Mother of God :

The Son of God, the eternal Son of the Father, when He became man, the illuminating Sun of the earth, the true light, selected for Himself a messenger who was to go before His face and proclaim the hour of His approach. In that harmony with which almighty God binds together the things of heaven and the things of earth, He selected the name of the woman who was to herald His coming and called her in Syriac Miriam, *the star rising in darkness;* hence we may apply to her as well as to St. John the prophecy of the Scripture, " like the morning star in the midst of the cloud: like the moon in the midst of her rays, like the sun when he shines, so did she shine in the temple of God: the promise of hope and of light."

When the beloved disciple of Our Lord, the evangelist, wrote the Apocalypse, in which he was privileged to stand at the very portals of heaven and see the glory of God's court, and look back before the mountains were formed, before the hills were set upon their bases, the veil was lifted from his eyes and he beheld, as he described, " a great sign which appeared in heaven: a woman clothed with the sun and the moon under her feet, and on her head a crown of twelve stars." This woman was Mary, the Queen of heaven, the Morning Star.

The Church applies to Mary the words of Holy Scripture: " I was set up from eternity, and of old before the earth was made; before the hills I was brought forth. He had not yet made the earth nor the rivers." Before an angel in heaven contemplated the perfections of adorable divinity, Mary occupied the first place in the mind, and in the designs of the eternal Father, robed with the glory of her divine Son, the moon beneath her feet, that is, this earth in which we live; she is the Queen of the universe, the Mother of its King, Jesus Christ. Every child of the human race is born in sin. David says of himself: " Behold, I was conceived in iniquities, and in sins did my mother conceive me." All human beings are in the same condition, but of Mary the Scriptures say: " Thou art all fair, O My love, and there is not a spot in thee." Mary was preserved from all sin, before her conception and in her conception.

How well the name of Morning Star befits her ! How beautiful, in our loneliness, the name of Mary falls on our ears! Mary came, and Jesus Christ the Son of God came with her.

The one great grace which Mary received then to prepare her for the incarnation of the Son of God was that from eternity she was in the mind of God a pure and holy creature ; that the devil should never have a claim on her, for never should she be in his power.

Jesus Christ coming to redeem a sinful race takes His body from that race, but it is united to His divinity and whatever comes in contact with that must also be holy; the Mother must of necessity be pure and immaculate. We know that when almighty God calls a creature to any dignity, or

to any office, He bestows on that creature graces
which are necessary to fulfil all the duties connected with the office. So we read of the prophet
Jeremias: "The word of the Lord came to me
saying, Before thou camest forth out of the womb
I sanctified thee and made thee a prophet unto
the nations." We read the same of the birth of St.
John the Baptist: he was sanctified before his birth
by Our Lord Himself, so as to show the dignity
of his calling, his worthiness to be the precursor
of the Redeemer. Therefore, the Almighty by
His prophet says: "The Lord possessed me in
the beginning of His ways, before He made anything from the beginning." Deprive Mary of the
grace of the Immaculate Conception, let the
slightest taint of sin come upon her, and she is
spoiled of her beauty ; like each one of us she
would be a sinful creature.

Mary's connection with the mystery of the incarnation may be considered in two ways; one in
relation to God, the other in relation to man. In
her relation to God, as soon as she was born into
this world, from the moment she raised her
virginal eyes to heaven, her sweet and pure relation with God began, and His gifts and graces
were showered upon her. The gifts that Mary
received were intended as a preparation for the

divine crowning grace, the gift of divine mater-
nity. Mary's graces began even before she was
born. In view of the high designs He had for
her, God began her life with a grace more grand
than ever before vouchsafed to human creature:
she was conceived free from the taint of original
sin. For Mary the mystery of the incarnation
was the great cause of her freedom from sin. Her
virginal bosom was the only home worthy of a
God. For four thousand years darkness over-
shadowed the world, and the face of God was hidden from His creatures in anger and aversion.
Now at length was the Morning Star to rise, the
forerunner of a glorious day when the Lord was
to be born. What great, beautiful, holy thoughts
could we not multiply on this subject—Mary the
Mother of God !

Joachim and Ann were the father and the
mother of the Blessed Virgin. They were a holy
couple and practised all the virtues, and almighty
God gave them special graces that they might live
lives which were the holier for the honor of their
daughter, Mary : they both have become great ad-
vocates before God in all our necessities. Catholic
people have taken up the devotion to St. Joachim
and St. Ann ; have cultivated it and propagated
it, so that at Brittany, in France, we see a great

pilgrimage to the good St. Ann, and on this side
of the Atlantic, in Canada, not far from Quebec,
some of that devotion has been transferred, which
brings hundreds of thousands of pious people to
these shrines. We, too, if we have the means, may
be tempted to make that pilgrimage some day
when we grow older; but we need not go so far,
for in New York there is a portion of the arm of
St. Ann in the Church of St. John the Baptist.
It is said that great miracles have occurred there
through the intercession of this saint. At any
rate, let us follow the example of pious people,
and when we have any necessities, spiritual ones
especially, let us ask the help of this good saint in
obtaining them for us: the intercession of a great
saint is very powerful before God, and we shall
more easily obtain what we need than if we relied
solely on our own prayers.

In the city of Nazareth there lived a man,
Joachim, who had married a girl of Bethlehem,
and both were of the tribe of David, and lived
in Nazareth, where they had their little home,
and served the Lord " with singleness of heart."
What they had of this world's goods they shared
with the poor, and for the maintenance of the
house of the Lord, and for His service. They
were getting old, and no child had yet blessed

their home, though they had prayed without
ceasing. It was an affliction which God had
placed on them for His own purposes. We are
told that at length the good Ann felt persuaded
that her tears and prayers were heard; they were
a worthy father and mother of the Mother of
Jesus ; their virtues were not to go unrewarded.
God took this holy couple and made use of them
for the purposes of His holy providence in regard
to His Son, who was about to come into the world
in the incarnation.

A child was born to them; the name of Mary
was given to her, and she was presented in the
Temple.

Direct thy glance, O Christian soul, to Mary
immaculate and learn the priceless value of innocence and freedom from sin. For although we are
conceived and born in sin, the great and miraculous sacrament of baptism cleanses us from it and
once more restores innocence to our souls, so that
when in the state of grace our hearts are the temples of the holy Trinity. Happy indeed is the
Christian soul which keeps intact its baptismal
innocence; happy the soul that through grace is
again under the influence of God. O, holy and
immaculate Virgin Mary! I fly to thee bathed
in tears of repentance, like an erring and contrite

child to the bosom of its mother.   Look with compassion on me ! Present my necessities to the adorable Child and obtain relief for me.

The Birth of the Blessed Virgin.

IT was about the beginning of the month Tisri, which is the first of the civil year of the Jews, that the holy Virgin came into this world. Her birth, like that of her divine Son, was humble; her parents were of the people, although descended from a long line of kings, and they led, to all appearances, an obscure life ; that Mystical Rose, whom St. John afterwards beheld clothed with the sun as with a radiant garment, was to be realized now. The cradle of the Queen of angels was not adorned with gold nor covered with the richly embroidered quilts of Egypt; it was the cradle of the common people of that country.

When eight days were over in the case of a female child, the relatives assembled in the home, and then a name was given to the new-born babe. Then, eighty days after the birth of a daughter, the Jewish woman was solemnly purified. She went to the Temple and there through the priest she offered up her child to God, according to the law of Moses, and made an offering of a lamb or a dove. The rich also made other offerings; the poor bought a pair of doves at the gates of the Temple for a very small sum of money. But the gratitude of the pious mother went still further than the customary sacrifice: she offered to the Lord a victim more pure, a dove more innocent than any which fell bleeding at the sacrifice; she laid at the foot of the altar of the Most High the child whom He had given her, and solemnly promised to bring back her daughter to the Temple and to consecrate her to the service of the holy place, as soon as her mind was capable of serving God.

The ceremony being finished, the holy couple made their way back to their own country. There it was that this child of benediction passed her early years, growing up like one of those lilies whose loveliness is praised by Jesus Christ, and which, as St. Bernard says, have "the odor of hope" about them.

The Scripture says nothing of the infancy of Mary, but is not this silence full of much subject for proper meditation? She was then already full of grace, so that her life had in it more of heaven than of earth. She was always in the presence of God, the love of God was the one absorbing thought of her life. In appearance like a child or a young girl, her manner was not much dif-

ferent from that of others of her age. But her
graces and her virtues grew every day ; like the
Lord Himself, of whom she was a perfect picture,
she grew in grace before God and man. All that
is said of good children, but in a superior degree,
were united in this little child Mary. She was the
model of good children: and as they begin to love
God early in life, so she served God with an angelic
purity. In her all virtues shone out with a perfect and harmonious lustre. Good children are
like bright stars on a dark night. How much
more did the virtues of this blessed child brighten
up the darkness of the world of her time ! Her
loveliness is beyond all comparison. The only
Child who surpasses Mary is the Infant Jesus.
Jesus is the Sun of Justice, Mary is a perfect reflection of that glory. Whatever we may imagine
of the Infant Jesus that is beautiful be not afraid
to apply to the child Mary. Satan must have
been struck with the virtues of this holy child
Mary: but he could not approach to do her harm,
for she was protected by almighty God. In Mary
there were no evil inclinations, no concupiscence,
nothing disturbed the serenity and peace of her
soul. The false attractions and false principles
of the world had no effect on her. Whether she
ate or drank, or amused herself, it was all for the

glory of God. She recognized God in His creation. She loved her parents, was as affectionate and tender to them as a child should be, she was ever ready to do them whatever service lay in her power. There was nothing in which she fell short of the expectations her parents had of her ; she fulfilled the duties of her station of life perfectly; whatever they wanted was done at once; whatever she was to learn, she acquired without delay. Sometimes she was saddened at the wickedness of the people of this world who forgot their God, who disobeyed His commands. She felt sympathy for these benighted people and interceded for them. Ah, she felt herself really an exile from the vision of God on earth. She sighed for the coming of the promised Redeemer who was to free the poor human race from the slavery of Satan and make them happy children of God. She knew that the Redeemer of mankind was soon to come, but when it was to be accomplished and what were the designs of God she knew not, but she continued to pray.

Mary's understanding, like the day in some favored regions, had scarcely a dawn, and shone out clearly from her earliest childhood. Her fervor and the wisdom of her discourse, at a period when other children still enjoy only a purely physical existence, made her parents judge that the time of their separation was near at hand; and when Joachim had offered to the Lord, for the third time since the birth of his daughter, the first-fruits of the crops and the fruits of his small inheritance, the husband and wife gratefully set out for Jerusalem, taking with them their beloved child, to deposit within the sacred precincts of the Temple their treasure which they had received from the God of Israel.

St. Ambrose says of Mary about this stage of her life, that " her charming exterior was but a transparent veil which disclosed all her virtues: and her soul, the noblest and purest ever created, after the soul of Jesus Christ, revealed itself fully in her looks. Her presence seemed to sanctify all about her, and the very sight of her was sufficient to detach the mind from earthly things."

Mary Retires to the Temple.

The Presentation of the Blessed Virgin.

THREE years had passed since the birth of
Mary, and she was beginning to show her intelligence.   Mary's heart sighed for the service of
God in retirement, her mind was then where her
treasure was.   Often in her innocent way would
she touch on the subject that she was dedicated
to the service of the Temple; she would innocently
ask whether the time was not come when she
might fulfil her irresistible desire and the promise
of her parents.   It was sad to think of this part-
ing.   But though no fonder heart than St. Ann's
ever beat in mother's breast, she submitted with
cheerfulness to the trial and was at once prepared
to offer up her daughter to the service of God.
Well she understood that this darling of her heart
was not altogether her own; she was only a charge
confided to her by Heaven to be brought up for
the honor of God and the salvation of the child.

She knew that it was divine Providence who four years previous had led her to pronounce this vow: and that now its fulfilment was required. She fully understood that the ways of Providence, although obscure and mysterious to our mortal eyes, always lead in the end to a good purpose. Mary would find in the Temple true happiness and every advantage of body and mind.

In this departure of Mary to the Temple there is a great source of serious thought for us all. We should consider with what cheerfulness we ought to make the sacrifice to God of anything we have promised ; and remember never lightly to make these promises nor lightly to break them. Do not forget that when children follow out their vocation they should as far as possible do so with the consent of their parents, who should be persuaded to agree to the wishes of their children, and be reconciled to the will of God.

Parents should learn that they must not oppose their children's vocation from mere selfish motives nor for an earthly purpose; but whatever it costs, even to the breaking of their hearts, they should look only to the glory of God. Here then is a great school of wisdom for all who have to decide a vocation. This is so important an act for the temporal, and especially the spiritual, welfare of

the human being that it should not be done lightly
or carelessly.

What a beautiful spectacle of devotion and self-
sacrifice we often witness in our generous
Catholics, young and old, especially when sons
and daughters of wealthy families, to whom the
world with all its attractions stands open, receiving the call from above, with true heroism enter
the ranks of the priesthood or sisterhood ! Like
Mary going to the Temple, they dedicate themselves to the service of God.

Having before them a journey of several days,
Joachim and Ann, with the child, descended the
woody slopes of Carmel into the charming plains
which extend between the mountains of Palestine
and the coasts of Syria, that fair region whose
climate is so mild that the orange tree blossoms in
the depth of winter. Along this route were groves
of palms, pomegranates, and the dark olive; water-
courses well supplied in winter with running water
and overhung by graceful willows. Now they were
about to ascend the hill on which stands Jerusalem, the city of God. Here all was changed : no
more flowers, but sterile rocks, deep ravines, with
few patches of land; the whole country one rocky
surface. On this stands the beautiful city of Jerusalem, the vision of God. There were enormous

towers, magnificent palaces, fortified citadels. There
stood the Temple of God, radiant with gold. So
thickly was the Temple covered with plates of gold
that when day began to appear it was no less daz-
zling than the rising sun. Let us take a nearer
view of this great Temple of God, the future home
of the Blessed Virgin. Our children, too, ought
to know a little something about it, for it will be
interesting and you will find that it will clear up
many things in the Scripture and the Catechism
that would otherwise be unintelligible.

A triple enclosure of massive stone walls with
ninety forts encompassed that singular city, and
all around it lay gloomy valleys, dizzy heights, and
inaccessible rocks. A stately and warlike city
which seemed as though it were transported by
magic from fabulous region; this is Jerusalem,
which even at the present day in its fallen state
is known as the " holy city," and is held in such
veneration that when pilgrims come to the place
and set foot on the ground for the first time they
prostrate themselves and kiss that sacred soil.

Having passed the magnificent gate, by which
they had to enter the city, Joachim and Ann found
themselves in the city of dark streets, bordered by
heavy-looking houses with very few windows.
There are not many windows in Eastern houses; air

is reached and breathed from the tops of houses, on the flat roofs of which the people enjoy themselves and are free from the turmoil of the busy streets. Within this city, on an elevation of Mount Moria, was the Temple. Its history takes up very much of the Scriptures, because they tell us, from the time of Moses to the building of the Temple, of all the regulations that were made for its erection, its maintenance, and repairs. The Temple of Jerusalem was the great holy place to which every Jew looked with fascination, and considered himself happy if he could say he had visited it once in his lifetime. That Temple had undergone many changes: it had been destroyed and rebuilt. Solomon made it beautiful, and the work of after times could not compare with his. This Temple was within the city and was surrounded by an outer wall; it had courtyards and enclosures. The enclosure of strangers or those who were not Jews ; enclosures where the cattle necessary for the sacrifice were kept, and several others for different uses. There was the porch of the Gentiles, where a Gentile, or one who was not a Jew, had to stop; it was death to go further. There was Solomon's porch ; there the great Jew and the pious Jew posed to be admired by the passers-by; there they met and made arrangements for union sacrifices for the benefit of a whole family.

From the middle of the Gentiles' porch arose two other enclosures, both sacred, which composed the Temple. The Temple was perfectly square, and ten gates gave access to the interior, where only Jews could be admitted. Jewish women could not enter a church either: even to the present day a woman must go to the galleries, or the enclosure for women, whilst a man, wearing a high hat, goes to the body of the synagogue. So in the Temple of Jerusalem there was a woman's enclosure. The sons and husbands could approach closer to the Holy of holies ; women prayed apart in upper galleries.

Of course the ceremony of the presentation took place in the woman's gallery: it was begun with a sacrifice. The priests and the Levites, assembled in the inner enclosure, received the victim from the hands of Joachim. The priest wore a turban of thick linen; he had on a tunic or a long garment, like our alb, held at the waist by a sky-blue cincture. One of the priests took the lamb and, after a short invocation, slaughtered it, turning his head towards the north; the blood was caught in a vase of brass and sprinkled around the Temple. These preliminary rites being per-

formed, a golden dish was arranged with a portion
of the flesh of the sacrifice. The priest wrapped the
oblation in a coat of fat, covered it with incense,
and sprinkled it with sacrificial salt; then, ascend-
ing barefoot the platform in front of the brazen
altar, he deposited the offering on the sound, firm
logs which fed the sacred fire. The remainder of
the animal, with the exception of the breast and
shoulders, which belonged to the priest, was given
back to the one who was offering the sacrifice, and
furnished meat for a banquet which was expected
by the friends who had come some distance and
had to be fed. In some cases the feast lasted even
longer than one day, and what was left over from
it was given to the poor.

The last sounds of the trumpet of the priest
had died away when he descended to the woman's
court in order to complete the ceremony. Ann,
followed by Joachim, and bearing Mary in her
arms, advanced, veiled, towards the minister of
the most high God, and said with a tremulous
voice: "I come to offer you the gift which God
gave me." The priest accepted, in the name of
God; then he extended his hands over the assem-
bly and prayed: "O Israel, may the Lord shed
His light upon thee : may He prosper thee in all
thy ways, and grant thee peace !" A canticle of

thanksgiving accompanied with harps terminated the presentation of the Virgin.

Such was the ceremony which took place towards the end of November in the holy Temple of Sion. Those who usually go no further than the surface saw there only a child of marvellous beauty and great piety, but the angels of heaven beheld in that fair creature the Virgin of whom Isaias spoke : she was the celestial Eve who came to restore to fallen man the hope of a happy immortality. The angels knew it from the revelation of God ; they thronged about that earthly festival and, covering that child with their snowy wings, celebrated with gladness, in union with the whole court of heaven, the solemn entry of the Blessed Virgin Mary into the Temple of Jerusalem.

The following verses may be aptly inserted here on the same subject:

> The light slants down the Temple-stair
> Upon an aged couple there,
> With quiet eyes and silvery hair.
>
> Between them, like a rosebud bright,
> And fresh and sweet, a child in white
> On either side a hand holds tight.
>
> She hath but three sweet summers told,
> That little girl with locks of gold,
> Between her parents grave and old;

Yet round her hidden angels say:
" Gloria tibi, Domine !
Our sovereign Queen is here to-day ! "

And while she marvels at the hymn,
Sweet Anne and gentle Joachim
Conduct her up the staircase dim.

The Golden Gate is open wide,
And, in and out, a surging tide,
The groups of strangers ceaseless glide.

But no one heeds the aged pair,
Or the infant with her sunny hair
(God's favorite friends forgotten fare).

And few behold the high priest stand
In his glittering vestments, old and grand,
With unrolled parchment in his hand,

Save little Mary, brave and sweet,
Who kneels before the rabbi's feet
And lisps the words his lips repeat.

She does not say: " O gracious King !
I'm but a little trembling thing,
Too weak to quit my mother's wing ! "

She does not plead: " O Lord divine !
Forbear, until I taste the wine
Of future joys which may be mine ! "

Nor still with cheeks and eyelids wet:
" My harvest is not ripened yet,
My zeal is mastered by regret ! "

But, firm and free and strong of nerve
(While radiant smiles the bright lips curve):
"Take all, O God: without reserve!"

And Anna feels her heart grow weak,
And Joachim is pale of cheek,
As the maiden, rising, turns to speak.

She stands between them, like a lamb,
She gives to each a tiny palm:
And says "Farewell!" in accents calm

And then it seems as dark as night,
As the Levite takes the child in white
And leads her slowly from their sight.

And angels shall her playmates be,
To guard the maiden on whose knee
Shall bloom the Incarnate Deity.

And after her (the prophets sing),—
Shall eager virgins following
Be brought with gladness to the King!

       —*Eleanor C. Donnelly*

Mary's Life in the Temple.

WITHIN the fortified enclosure of the Temple was an edifice set apart for virgins consecrated to God, who busied themselves in the service of the altar in every needful manner. Thither the child was conducted.

Virginity was not held in the sacred light in which it is esteemed now; it was not considered a perpetual vow, and sooner or later those consecrated to it were released in order to enter an honorable marriage. Still those who engaged in the solemn vow were not without honors and special prerogatives. God must have delighted in the prayers of these spotless children, who were guarded against the approach of all sin. The institution of virgins about the Temple was a very ancient one: we may refer back to the time of Moses when his sister Mary with other maidens chanted the praises of God who had liberated their fathers from the bondage of Pharao. We find them mentioned in several passages of the Scriptures, so that we may conclude that the same institution continued in the time of Mary. Whatever may be said to the contrary it appears pretty certain that there were virgins attached to the service of the second Temple at the time of Mary's presentation, and that she was enrolled among them. The institutions of the first Christians certify to the fact and several of the Fathers refer to it. The education which Mary received in the Temple was the best that the times and customs of the Hebrews supplied. It was chiefly confined to the domestic labors which in all well-regulated homes are done by the daughters of the family. Brought up in the strict observance of the Mosaic law they went early to the prayers prescribed. "Let Thy name, O Lord, be praised and glorified in this world, which Thou hast created according to Thy pleasure; vouchsafe to establish Thy reign, let redemption flourish, and the Messias come quickly." And the people assembled for morning prayers would answer, "Amen." Having fulfilled this sacred duty of the morning, they engaged themselves in work: spinning, embroidering, and all the arts of working in wool, interweaving it with threads of gold. They were also taught to read the sacred Scriptures, for they were

to know all that pertained to their religion and
to the practice of it in every ceremony in which
they were concerned.

St. Bonaventure gives us the following order of
the day, as passed by this chosen daughter of
heaven: "Mary spent in prayer and meditation
the first hours of the day, from dawn till nine
o'clock. From nine till three in the afternoon she
was occupied with manual labor and in reading
the Holy Scriptures. She then attended the evening sacrifice offered daily in the Temple, after
which she partook of food brought to her." Thus
manual occupation alternated with spiritual
duties. When we remember the large number of
priests whose rich and varied vestments were to
be made, repaired, and kept in good order; and
then again the vast amount of draperies and other
articles used at the sacrifices and other ceremonies,
we may form some idea of the many duties devolv-
ing upon these young virgins. It is an ancient
tradition, handed down from mother to daughter,
that the Blessed Virgin surpassed all her companions in the artistic work required of her. In
proof of her excellence in useful work it is said
that she afterwards wove the seamless garment
worn by Jesus when a boy, and which was
miraculously enlarged as He grew up to youth and

manhood. Every principle of knowledge and piety, every lesson of sacred history which she received from her teachers, was so indelibly imprinted on her memory, forming in their entirety such a treasure of holy and spiritual knowledge as was never before granted to human mind, that she might even then be justly called the " Seat of Wisdom." Then we think, perhaps very justly, that this knowledge was increased by frequent revelations from God.

But not only was this retirement in the Temple an opportunity for manual training: how much more rapid must have been her advancement in virtue and the perfection of her soul! St. Alphonsus tells us of Mary's youth: " As the breaking dawn of the morning becomes brighter, as the perfect day approaches, so did Mary grow more perfect in every accomplishment; no pen can describe the increasing brilliancy of her virtues, her humility, her silence, self-denial, and her gentleness." St. Jerome says: " Mary was the most prompt of her companions, the most faithful in the observance of the divine law, the humblest and yet the most perfect in the practice of every virtue. She was never known to be angry, and her every word breathed gentleness, mildness, and heavenly love: so that, by every word and action the observer was reminded of God." St. Ambrose writes of her youth in a similar strain: "Mary said but little, was always recollected, did not laugh boisterously, and was so retiring and reserved as never to thrust herself upon the notice of others. With constancy and perseverance she practised prayer, fasting, and the study of the Scriptures and other useful occupations."

These are beautiful descriptions of the mind and heart of Mary: they come from saints of God who knew what one ought to be who was so very dear to the Almighty: let us insert here one more testimony of St. Ambrose, who says: " She was a virgin in heart and soul as well as in body, and never permitted the shadow of evil to cloud her purity for a moment. In disposition humble, in conversation guarded, careful in her thoughts, sparing of her words, attentive in her reading and instructions. She censured none, loved all, respected old age, was a stranger to jealousy and envy, shunned vanity, and loved to commune with her Creator. She did not allow her eyes to wander, she never dropped a useless word, or did a dishonorable action. Her movements were free from vanity, her carriage modest, her voice soft and gentle. This excellent maiden discharged all her duties with such a perfect consciousness that she seemed by her beautiful example in every virtue to be rather the preceptress than the pupil."

Thus we may well conceive that never since the beginning of creation was a more delightful object presented to the entranced gaze of the angels, nor even to the Deity itself than the immaculate and richly endowed heart of Mary with its thousand blooming flowers of fragrant virtue.

We have dwelt so long on the child Mary because her life is such a near approach to Our Lord's life; there is no question that when we describe Mary's childhood we may consider that the youthful life of Jesus, to which this book is devoted, is described at the same time, only, of course, that we must make His life divine, whilst that of Mary was a holy life produced by the grace of God. This contemplation of the life of Mary will also have another effect. It will teach parents and those who have the care of the education of girls in their hands what the life of girls ought to be in this world. Girls nowadays are well brought up too, and have magnificent opportunities of learning history, geography, reading, etc. This ought not to be all: the heart and the soul need to be educated too; they must also imbibe with the secular accomplishments those virtues which make good Catholic girls. They will have to learn humility, gentle docility, childlike obedience, and virginal purity of soul: all other accomplishments will not be real education if these are wanting. When the age of girlhood is passed they will become capricious, selfish, indolent, morose, unfaithful to all their duties unless there is the backing of real, solid virtue. Too late will parents and the young woman victim find out the falsity of her education. Hence, happy are the parents who have not permitted themselves to be misled by outward show, worldly vanity, but who have set before their eyes the story of the life and childhood of Mary.

Such parents will find in their old age comfort in their children; they will have a good home with them, they will be cared for to the end of their days, they will feel that their age is not a burden to their children, and that the room which they occupy in their last days is not begrudged to them. This is the effect of the education of the heart ; who will say that mere secular education is preferable ?

Whilst the Blessed Virgin was passing her days in the service of God in the Temple her parents retired to Nazareth, their town, and there lived in peace and quiet, remembering their sweet daughter Mary. From time to time Ann and

Joachim would go to Jerusalem for the celebration of the festivals of the Jewish year, and on these occasions surely they also sought to look upon their good child and spend a few hours with her. But Mary's parents were getting old and their death was approaching. What is more natural than to suppose that Mary, making a sacrifice of her inclination for the glory of God and to show her filial duty to her parents, went to their bedside and made herself useful ? What happiness did not this young girl bring to her parents ! Happy indeed were these parents to see their beloved child once more : what holy and religious sentiments did not Mary breathe into their ears ? They died in the arms of her who was one day to be the Mother of God. For us, too, the tender love of Mary for her departing parents is a source of much consolation. We know that this Blessed Virgin never abandons in the hour of death those who have been true to her in life. The last moment of our life decides our eternity. In this last solemn moment the devil will not cease his endeavors to weaken our faith or extinguish our love for God. But Mary, who is so faithful to her duties, will not leave the bedside of those who have served her through life and who at that moment call on her for assistance. As she acted so tenderly to her mother and father so she will also be to us our consolation and our hope. "Thus," as St. Augustine observes, "the repentant sinner ascends to his Saviour through her through whom the Saviour had descended to him."

O, Blessed Virgin, sweet Mother of mercy, I conjure thee by thy tender love that thou wilt come to my soul's assistance when my last hour shall have struck; put into my heart the thought of saying for the last time with my last breath, "Jesus, Mary, Joseph."

The Marriage of the Blessed Virgin.

At the proper time, at what age we know not, it was necessary, according to Jewish law, to look for a spouse for Mary. In those Eastern climes a young girl arrives much earlier at a marriageable age than in our more vigorous northern country. The maidens who had dedicated themselves to the service of the Temple were not to remain single and be virgins all their life; it was customary to look for husbands for them. There was no courtship; there were laws by which they were guided and that directed them in making their choice. So the tribes kept to themselves as much as possible, as also did the families of the tribes. Mary shuddered at the mere thought of going forth into the great world; she persistently refused to enter into any relations with the many suitors that presented themselves, saying that she had made a vow of virginity and was desirous that it should hold. However, her resolve to remain a virgin seemed opposed to the law of Moses: it was considered sinful to permit a family to become extinct. Mary was the last of her family and she was therefore not considered at liberty to follow her own inclination ; her prayer was refused, and she was compelled to submit to the law. When the young men of the family of David, who had been invited to choose a wife, had assembled, the high priest directed them to do as Moses had once been inspired to do on another occasion. He requested each of the young men to hand him a dry rod. These the priest laid together on the altar before the Holy of holies, and then besought the Lord that He would cause the rod belonging to the young man intended as Mary's future husband to become green and to sprout and put forth leaves. When the priest returned on the following day to examine the twigs he found them dead and dry. The priests inquired whether, of the few descendants of the royal family, any had failed to take part in the ceremony, and it was found that a poor carpenter, named Joseph, had absented himself. This man had from early boyhood led a pure and holy life in the fear and wisdom of God, and like the Blessed Virgin had resolved to remain unmarried. This good man was at once ordered to the Temple, and, like the others, to bring with him a twig to be laid upon the altar. In

a short time the rod of this man became green,
sprouted and bore a beautiful lily. All saw the
miracle, and all acknowledged that he was the
man chosen by God to be the bridegroom for the
maiden of Nazareth. When the guardians an-
nounced to Mary the result of the scrutiny, she
hesitated not a moment to devote herself to an
obscure life, menial occupations, and arduous cares
with the humble artisan Joseph. Probably she
had been admonished from on high that this just
man would be to her a protector, a father, and the
guardian of her chastity. Our Lord had heard
her prayer. God gave not to His chosen daughter
a man whose merit consisted in the possession of
great lands, vineyards, or wealth: He had given
her a just man, the most perfect of His works; before Him there is no distinction between poor and
rich. "Man judges by appearances, but Jehovah
looks at the heart," says the Scripture. Joseph
possessed treasures of grace and of sanctity
which the angels themselves might envy; his
virtues had made him first among his people, and
his name stood far higher in the book of life than
that of the imperial Cæsar. The Virgin was not
confided to the most powerful, but to the most
worthy: thus the ark, which the princes and cap-
tains of Israel dared not touch for fear of being

stricken with death, drew down the blessing of
Heaven on the house of a simple Levite wherein it
was sheltered.

We are not inclined to believe that the marriage
of the Blessed Virgin was a great affair, for poor
people have to be content with a very modest ceremony. But it may be interesting to take a glance
at a Jewish marriage according to the customs of
that people, of which, no doubt, they all wished
to avail themselves.

Early in the morning a train of richly dressed
women approach the home of the bride, and slaves
carry torches as far as the house. Those who are
to take part in the ceremony are allowed to enter
to congratulate the bride on the blessing received
from God in the fact that a husband and protector
has been given her. Then begins the work of
adorning the bride; gold and pearls are lavished
upon her, bracelets and earrings, according to
Eastern custom, forming a necessary part of the
adornment: a pointed golden crown is set on her
brow; a bridal veil covers her from head to foot,
like a cloak. At the door of the house a canopy of
precious stuffs awaits her, and under it she and her
attendants have to walk. When the procession
begins to move, the nuptial train is lengthened out
by people who carry palm branches, waving them

as if in triumph and to show the joy of all. The procession moves on to the sound of cymbals, harps, and flutes. Then comes the bridegroom, his brow adorned with a peculiar crown of crystal. He is surrounded by a number of friends singing portions of the Canticle of Solomon. Young people who bring up the rear perform a religious dance and burst into prolonged cries of joy, as is still done at the present day by the Arabs. The whole procession, as it passes along, scatters small coin among the poor that line the roadside. Arrived at the future dwelling of the couple, the friends of the bride and groom sing in chorus to welcome them. Then the groom takes his station under the canopy, at the side of his bride, and places the wedding ring on her finger. One of the relatives then pours out a goblet of wine, which the young couple taste first, and then the groom pours the rest on the ground as a token of liberality, whilst those who are provided with it cast handfuls of wheat about as a sign of abundance. The king of the feast is then chosen; his duty is to see that the guests do not infringe the rules of religion or propriety. All then enter the banquet hall, where the feast lasts a long time; several days, in fact, the guests remain partaking of the hospitality of the house where the marriage has taken place. After the ceremony the bride and groom are considered lawfully married, and they can no longer separate except by a decree of the holy council.

Humble was perhaps the marriage of the Blessed Virgin, and with as little display as possible, because it was more becoming to the condition of poverty in which both Mary and Joseph found themselves.

After the festive days of the wedding were over, Mary with deep regret bade farewell to the Temple, whose sacred walls had so long sheltered her. She took leave of her companions, who were practising the virtue of chastity; and of her beloved and venerable preceptress, the prophetess Anna; of the pious and dear priests whose teachings of the law had been so useful to her. Fortified by the blessings of their friends, and the good wishes of all, the holy couple went to Nazareth to live in a poor home which was their own. Here Mary lived in the practice of the purest chastity with her spouse St. Joseph, who was himself strengthened by almighty God's grace to remain as he always had been, a virginal man. Here they loved each other, with God ever present to their minds; they prayed together, and St. Joseph labored for his wife. Each succeeding day St. Joseph became

more and more convinced that God had entrusted
to his care a priceless jewel. He could say of her,
according to Solomon: "I preferred her before
kingdoms and thrones, and esteemed riches as
nothing in comparison of her: gold in comparison
of her is as a little sand, and silver in respect to
her shall be counted as clay. I loved her above
health and beauty, and chose to have her instead
of light, for her light cannot be put out."

The Annunciation.

WE see that Mary's preparation for the great mystery of the incarnation was now complete. She shone in transcendent beauty like a being of paradise rather than a creature of this world. She was filled with supernatural virtues, she was the fitting shrine to which God could descend. O Mary, O marvellous, mystical creature whom God has now so completely formed to be the holy temple of His sacred presence ! What was it in Mary that so attracted God's complacency ? What drew the Word from the bosom of the Father into her bosom ? God saw in Mary His own great power and wisdom: it was all His work: He fell in love with His own wisdom when He loved her. Her natural life was His own idea; her beauty an expression of His own wisdom; her birth an act of His own almighty will. There was nothing in Mary that she had not received from God.

The place where the Son of God was to assume His created human nature was the inner room of the holy house of Nazareth, where Mary and Joseph dwelt together.

From the Gospel narrative it would appear that Mary had received no warning of what was about to happen, still less of the time when the mystery was to be accomplished. Mary was spending the time in closest union with God; her spirit was doubtless then raised in ecstasy to the raptures of contemplation. It was this prayer perhaps that hastened the time of the glorious mystery of the incarnation. It was perhaps her intense aspiration, into which she threw her whole soul, that drew the everlasting Word from the bosom of the Father.

Before the Son of God came Himself He sent His messenger before Him in the person of the angel Gabriel, the angel of the incarnation. Gabriel had been, as we read, the official herald of the decrees of God regarding the incarnation. The works of Daniel's prophecy had now run out, and the messenger was at hand to ask in the name of God Mary's consent, and for a moment the accomplishment hung on Mary's word. The visit is thus described by St. Luke the Evangelist: " In the sixth month the angel Gabriel was sent from God into a city of Galilee, called Nazareth, to a virgin espoused to a man whose name was Joseph, of the house of David, and the Virgin's name was Mary. And the angel being come in said unto her: Hail full of grace; the Lord is with thee; blessed art thou amongst women. Who having heard was troubled at his saying, and thought with herself what manner of salutation this should be. And the angel said to her: Fear not, Mary, for thou hast found grace with God: behold thou shalt conceive in thy womb, and shalt bring forth a Son, and thou shalt call His name Jesus. He shall be great, and shall be called the Son of the Most High, and the Lord God shall give unto Him the throne of David, His father, and He shall reign in the house of Jacob forever : and of His kingdom there shall be no end. And Mary said to the angel: How shall this be done, because I know not man ? And the angel answering said to her: The Holy Ghost shall come upon thee and the power of the Most High shall overshadow thee. And therefore also the Holy which shall be born of thee shall be called the Son of God. And behold thy cousin Elizabeth, she also hath conceived a son in her old age: and this is the sixth month with her that is called barren: because no word shall be impossible with God."

What a salutation is this ! There was joy in the words of the angel; he brings joyful news from the throne of God. O, most holy Virgin, I salute thee with all my heart, he says, for the Lord God has thought of thee, has had thee in His mind, and I am come to speak to thee of it.

Thou art full of grace : the friend of God full of charity, faith, and hope; full of the perfect practice of all virtues: humility, obedience, patience; thou art full of wisdom, knowledge, piety, and the fear of the Lord and all the virtues consequent on the gifts of the Holy Ghost. Her memory is full of holy thoughts, her intelligence full of God's mercy, her will is entirely conformable to the will of God that the world might be redeemed and that soon the Messias should come. Mary is full of grace in her actions for the glory of God; her life was full of good works, all directed by the proper intention for the love of God. Every day Mary was still receiving: the measure was being filled up, heaped up and pressed down.

And why was this greatness of the mercy of God poured out on her—the Lord is with thee. He is thy friend, O Mary, Mother of God, He is with thee in every faculty of thy soul, He is with thee in His holy and watchful providence, He is with thee forever. O, glorious Virgin, how great art thou when the Lord is with thee ! when He is thy friend, thy spouse, thy Father: thou art by

this relation all powerful with the Lord. Mary
is the mistress of the treasures of the graces of
almighty God which we need so much; no greater
gift could this woman full of grace give us than
to send us a share of her fulness of grace. We
need that mysterious strength from above, by
which our understanding is enlightened, our hearts
inflamed with love for the good and the spiritual,
which awakens in us the desire of Christian virtue, making its practice easy. Thus it is that the
fulness of grace of Mary has been a great benefit
to the human race; the Lord is with Mary, with
Him she comes to us blessing us, sympathizing
with us, praying for us. Mary has become our
refuge in this valley of tears. O clement, O loving, O sweet Virgin Mary ! Pray for us that we
may be worthy of the promises of Christ.

Hence she is the most blessed among women;
never was there such a woman on earth, never did
God create circumstances in which such a woman
was possible. All saintly women of the Old and
the New Testament dwindle into insignificance in
comparison with this woman, blessed among
women. The possession of God made her great,
the fulness of grace made her great, and no other
woman was blessed to such an extent. Blessed
art thou among women, and blessed is the fruit of

thy womb, Jesus, the Son of God, the Son of the Most High. "I am appointed King over Sion. The Lord hath said to Me: Thou art My Son, this day have I begotten Thee: ask of Me and I will give Thee the Gentiles for Thy inheritance and the utmost parts of the earth for Thy possession."

In woman man was one time accursed, but by Mary has blessing come not only to women but to all the human race. Eve listened to the serpent and ruined the happiness of the whole human race forever. Mary crushed the head of the serpent. No wonder then that the salutation of the angel astonished Mary, for the promises of the angel opened up such a sublime future that the holy Virgin in her humility could not comprehend it.

No wonder that Mary was astonished and disturbed at such words coming from a visitor whom she did not know. She showed by her disturbance her great humility, for she was a sensible woman, and knew that she could not be specially distinguished among women. She knew that she was unknown and married to a poor carpenter; why should she become so famous throughout the world that all women should call her blessed? When the angel saw Mary's concern **at** his presence he sweetly

and gently soothed her by his speech : Fear not,
Mary; for you have found grace before God. Be
not afraid, there is no harm coming to you: no
misfortune or violence is coming over you: fear
not, Mary, you will not commit sin, the devil will
have no power over you. God is your protector,
you have found grace with God; His strong arm
is raised in your defence.

When the angel had allayed the fears of the
Virgin he proceeded to lay before her the designs
God had for her, that the Messias was to be born,
that she was to be the instrument of God's providence, to introduce His Son into the world ; she
was to be His Mother, to conceive Him, bear
Him in her bosom for nine months, and that then
He should be born. "Behold, thou shalt conceive in thy womb and shalt bring forth a Son
and thou shalt call His name Jesus. He shall be
great and shall be called the Son of the Most
High: and the Lord God shall give Him the
throne of His father David, and He shall reign
in the house of Jacob forever, and of His kingdom
there shall be no end." Here, then, is what God
has designed in the life of Mary: she is a privileged creature to be the Mother of the Son of the
Most High. She shall be great. Who is greater
than the Son of God ? His reign will have no

end: all over the world His power will extend; as long as the world will last Jesus will be adored.

This is the Son of whom Isaias speaks in the Old Testament when he says : " A Child is born to us, and a Son is given to us : and the government is upon His shoulder, and His name shall be called Wonderful, Counsellor, God, the Mighty, the Father of the world to come, the Prince of peace. He shall sit upon the throne of David, and upon His kingdom."

" How shall this be done ? " inquired Mary, "because I know not man." The prudent virgin did not ask out of want of faith nor from mistrust in God's goodness, but rather out of solicitude for her life's resolve to remain chaste. From this fact she is called most prudent Virgin, because she wished to be more fully instructed so as to guard her innocence. She became an example to us all in this, showing us that we should prudently, carefully avoid every danger to our purity, be circumspect, and not permit ourselves to be led astray by the devil, even though he appear in the garb of an angel of light. Then the angel, to show her that she would not lose her virginity in becoming the Mother of the Son of God, tells her that God would effect all by the power of the holiest, purest Spirit. He answered:

" The Holy Ghost shall come upon thee, and the power of the Most High shall overshadow thee : and therefore also the Holy which shall be born of thee shall be called the Son of God." Thou shalt always be a pure virgin, God wills it that thy purity shall always be guarded ; thou shalt be the purest of virgins.

And to show Mary that God's power is very great and that strange things were happening just then in preparation for the coming of the Messias, the angel refers to a secret which nobody knew among the relatives—that Elizabeth, an old woman, had conceived a son in her old age, for nothing is impossible to God. The whole plan of almighty God had now been laid before the Virgin, that she might act upon it and decide what she would do. The messenger was waiting there to carry the answer back to the throne of God. Mary, with the grace of God, had made up her mind, and gave her consent. It meant much for her to do this, for there were disgrace, poverty, and desertion staring her in the face. She could foresee what happened afterwards, the doubts of St. Joseph in regard to his wife's faithfulness. But humbly bowing to the will of God, Mary answered: " Behold the handmaid of the Lord, be it done to me according to

thy word." As if to say, What am I, but a poor
miserable creature, worth nothing, incapable of
doing anything? let Him take His servant and
make use of her according to His designs; a poor
handmaid, the lowliest of His earthly creatures.
I shall be submissive, I will do whatever is required of me. This was the great act of obedience
in the life of Mary. Often she had to practise
humility and obedience, but on this occasion the
depths of the virtue, or rather the sublimity of
it, were reached. "Be it done to me according
to thy word." And the angel departed from her.
With joy this messenger of God ascended to
heaven to report to the choirs of God's angels the
fulfilment of his mission; and then all the angels
rejoiced for the mercy of God which was to be
shown to man.

The salutation of the angel, my dear children,
is often repeated: not a day of our life passes but
we repeat in prayer the words of the *Hail Mary*.
Many times we multiply the recital of it when
we say the beads; we never go to bed at night
or rise in the morning that we do not say it gladly;
and we repeat it daily at every action of our life.
So we often remind the Blessed Virgin that we
are thinking of her; that we salute her with the
salutation of the angel, to recall that first saluta-

tion; that we rejoice over it no less than the angels do in heaven; that we love that Virgin and hail her also as blessed among all women.

The Birth of St. John Foretold.

WE have just heard that the angel referred to
the fact that St. Elizabeth, a cousin of the Blessed
Virgin, had by the power of God, by a special
providence, conceived and was soon to give birth
to a real prodigy. The story is wonderful, and
we shall present it just as it appears in the New
Testament, in the Gospel of St. Luke : "There
was in the days of Herod, the king of Judea, a
certain priest named Zachary, of the course of
Abia, and his wife was of the daughters of Aaron,
and her name Elizabeth. And they were both
just before God, walking in all the commandments
and justifications of the Lord without blame, and
they had no son, for that Elizabeth was barren,
and they both were well advanced in years. And
it came to pass, when he executed the priestly
function in the order of his course before God,
according to the custom of his priestly office, it
was his lot to offer incense, going into the Temple
of the Lord. And all the multitude of the people

was praying without at the hour of incense. And
there appeared to him an angel of the Lord, standing on the right side of the altar of incense. And
Zachary, seeing him, was troubled, and fear fell
upon him. But the angel said to him: Fear not,
Zachary, for thy prayer is heard, and thy wife
Elizabeth shall bear thee a son, and thou shalt
call his name John. And thou shalt have joy
and gladness, and many shall rejoice in his nativ-
ity. For he shall be great before the Lord, and
shall drink no wine nor strong drink, and he shall
be filled with the Holy Ghost even from his
mother's womb. And he shall convert many of
the children of Israel to the Lord their God. And
he shall go before Him in the spirit and power of
Elias, that he may turn the hearts of the fathers
unto the children, and the incredulous to the wisdom of the just, to prepare unto the Lord a perfect
people. And Zachary said to the angel : Whereby
shall I know this ? for I am an old man and my
wife is advanced in years. And the angel answering said to him : I am Gabriel, who stand before
God, and am sent to speak to thee and to bring
thee these good tidings. And behold, thou shalt
be dumb, and shalt not be able to speak until the
day wherein these things shall come to pass, because thou hast not believed my words, which shall

be fulfilled in their time. And the people was waiting for Zachary, and they wondered that he tarried so long in the Temple. And when he came out, he could not speak to them, and they understood that he had seen a vision in the Temple. And he made signs to them, and remained dumb. And it came to pass, after the days of his office were accomplished, he departed to his own house. And after those days Elizabeth his wife conceived, and hid herself five months, saying: Thus hath the Lord dealt with me in the days wherein He hath had regard to take away my reproach among men."

The offices of the several priests, who were appointed to the service of the Temple on the successive days during which their class was in attendance, were arranged by lot. Probably the most solemn of all, and never intermitted, were those which had direct relation to the daily sacrifice of the lamb, morning and evening, and of offering incense on the golden altar in the holy place. Here, too, stood the golden candlestick of seven branches, whose lamps were continually burning before the veil which shrouded the Holy of holies from the gaze of men, and here were the loaves of proposition renewed once a week by the priests whose office it was to attend to them. The holy place was hidden by a curtain from the rest of the Temple, and thus when the priest went in to perform his solemn office, the devout worshippers could only follow him with their hearts and pray earnestly for the continuance of the blessings with which God was ever defending and enlightening His people. Into the Holy of holies itself, which was separated from the holy place by a veil, no one ever entered except the high priest once a year, on the great Day of Atonement. The sacred text tells us that on the occasion when Zachary entered, the whole multitude was praying without at the time of the incense. The priest was to enter the Holy of holies with a vessel filled with incense and scatter the incense on the sacred fire of the altar. After the offering of the incense, the priest was to return to the sight of the people and dismiss them with the solemn blessing, saying : " The Lord bless thee and keep thee; the Lord show His face to thee and have mercy on thee; the Lord turn His countenance to thee and give thee peace." It was at just such a ceremony that the miraculous appearance of the angel took place, which is related by St. Luke. The appearance, too, of the angel in the Temple at this solemn moment and in the Holy of holies conveyed a meaning intended not only for Zachary, but for all present. In fact

the Messias was soon to come; this appearance
of the angel was a necessary prelude to its realiza-
tion, and the people were to be informed that the
kingdom of God was at hand. This child that is
to be born will bring joy to the heavenly hosts,
to the souls of the patriarchs and other saints of
the Old Testament, for he is as the dawn of the
glorious day of the redemption of mankind for
which they have so eagerly waited. The reason
for this joy is that the child "shall be great before the Lord" with a greatness which God alone
can give : great in sanctity, great in the office he
will fill in the kingdom of the Messias to which he
will belong. To prepare him for his mission he
was to be consecrated by the vow of the Nazarenes,
a solemn consecration which was frequently under-
taken for a time or for life, as in the case of St.
John. "He shall drink no wine nor strong drink."
This consecration of the child was to be the preparation for the wonderful graces bestowed on his
soul, for "he shall be filled with the Holy Ghost
even from his mother's womb." This, my dear
children, was a special privilege of the precursor,
his sanctification before his birth. This sanctification by the Holy Ghost from his mother's womb
is not promised as a thing which once given remains, but it means that it shall increase with the

years of his life. "And he shall convert many of the children of Israel to the Lord their God." The office of the Baptist was to prepare the people for the coming of the Messias, to fit them to receive His spiritual gifts by their conversion from sin. He was also to point Him out to them that they might listen to Him more readily: he was to introduce Him to them that they might know Him. Thus the greatness of St. John was predicted, and the grace of God was given to him to go forth on his mission.

Zachary was so long within the enclosure of the Holy of holies that it was evident something extraordinary had happened to him, for the people were waiting to be dismissed with the invocation of the blessing. They wondered that he tarried so long. When he came out he could not speak to them, and they understood that he had seen a vision in the Temple. St. Elizabeth retired from public view and hid herself; thus the weeks and months which were to pass before the birth of the child were to become a time of prayer, penance, and thanksgiving to God for His favors, in which she joined her husband as penance for his incredulity.

The Visitation.

WHEN Mary had been informed by the angel of the miraculous pregnancy of St. Elizabeth she resolved to go and offer her tender congratulations to her venerable relative. It was not because she doubted the words of the angel, or to assure herself by ocular demonstration, that she resolved on this visit, for she knew that nothing is impossible to God and that His words are the truth. So she set out with haste, so as to be of service as early as possible; with her wonted kindness and benevolence she longed to impart a portion of that blessing which now sprang from her presence.

> Whither thus, in holy rapture,
>   Royal maiden, art thou bent?
> Why so fleetly art thou speeding
>   Up the mountain's rough ascent?
>
> Filled with the eternal Godhead!
>   Glowing with the Spirit's flame!
> Love it is that bears thee onward
>   And supports thy tender frame.

Blessed Mother! joyful meeting!
  Thou in her, the hand of God,
She in Thee, with lips inspired,
  Owns the Mother of her Lord.

Honor, glory, virtue, merit,
  Be to Thee, O Virgin's Son!
With the Father and the Spirit
  While eternal ages run.

Alone she went into the mountains of Judea, a
five days' journey. Probably on her journey Mary
found companions among those who constantly
travelled to the holy city and thus a great portion
of the road was made under their protection. Arrived at length at the sacerdotal town, Mary went
straight to the house of Elizabeth. On seeing her
approach, the Virgin bowed down and laying her
hands on her heart, as was then the customary mode
of salutation, exclaimed, " Peace be with you ! "
Elizabeth drew back; joy and friendly recognition
were in her face, but profound respect marked her
external greeting. Suddenly the prophetic spirit descended upon her and she cried out, " Blessed art
thou among women and blessed is the fruit of thy
womb. And whence is this to me, that the Mother
of my Lord should come to me ? For behold as
soon as the voice of thy salutation sounded in my
ears the infant in my womb leaped for joy. And

blessed art thou that hast believed, because those
things shall be accomplished that were spoken to
thee by the Lord." Then Mary answered with the
beautiful canticle: " My soul doth magnify the
Lord, and my spirit hath rejoiced in God my Saviour. Because He hath regarded the humility of
His handmaid : for behold from henceforth all
generations shall call me blessed. Because He that
is mighty hath done great things to me : and holy
is His name. And His mercy is from generation
to generations, to them that fear Him. He hath
showed might in His arm : He hath scattered the
proud in the conceit of their heart. He hath put
down the mighty from their seat and hath exalted
the humble. He hath filled the hungry with good
things and the rich He hath sent empty away. He
hath received Israel His servant, being mindful
of His mercy. As He spoke to our fathers, to
Abraham and to his seed forever." " In this celebrated interview," says St. Ambrose, " Mary and
Elizabeth both prophesied by the Holy Ghost, for
both were filled with the Holy Spirit by the merit
of their children."

Mary remained three months with her cousin St.
Elizabeth. How pure, how sublime must have
been the discourse of these two holy women: one
about to become the Mother of God ; the other

the mother of the precursor of the Son of God: both profoundly loving God, and both well pleasing to almighty God. The mild and amiable Virgin lavished on Elizabeth all her kindest attentions : they were just such as Mary would have bestowed on her own mother, and we may suppose that she was often reminded of her own parents by the sight of that loving and devoted pair, who loved her so tenderly and with a parental care, and treated her with profound respect. It is easy to imagine that many were the blessings which descended on the house of Zachary through the visit of the Blessed Virgin. We recall the blessings which Obededom received from the presence of the ark of the covenant in his house, even so as to excite the envy of the holy king David ; what blessings, then, must not Zachary have received from the three months' sojourn of Mary, who is the ark of the new covenant ?

On Mary's return to Nazareth she cheerfully resumed her former mode of life. She became again the active and diligent housewife, who finds time for work, for prayer, and for pious reading: whose whole conversation was in heaven, and who seemed to have applied to herself those beautiful words of the Psalmist: " All the glory of the king's daughter is within."

Nearer and nearer approached the time for our
dear Saviour's coming, and St. Joseph, the spouse
of the Virgin, became every day more sad and
downcast; he was as yet ignorant of the work of
God in her, and he was very much disturbed.
" She was found with child," says the Gospel.
What was he to do in his perplexity ? According to the law of Moses adultery was punishable
by death. A hasty, passionate husband would
not have failed to drag his wife before the priests
of the Lord, that sentence should be passed upon
her. But Joseph would not take such a step :
he knew too well that Mary was innocent, that
she was purity itself : and being a just man,
he was unwilling to expose her and was about to
put her away secretly. Mary could not but notice
the deep concern that Joseph manifested; it must
have caused her great grief to conceal from him
the glorious embassy of the angel. But how was
she to speak to Joseph about it ? She hoped in
God, she trusted that in due time He would reveal
to Joseph what great things He was doing through
Mary. " The daughter of David," says the great
Bishop of Meaux, " at the risk of seeing herself
not only suspected and abandoned, but also lost
and dishonored, left all to God and remained in
peace." God did send an angel to Joseph, who

said, " Fear not to take unto thee Mary thy wife :
for that which is conceived in her is of the Holy
Ghost." Joseph's doubts disappeared at once ; his
great faith needed no other proof ; his sorrow
changed to joy. He made amends for having
doubted his spouse, and Mary thanked God for His
protection. The good St. Joseph redoubled his
efforts towards his virginal spouse ; it was now
he showed the full extent of his vocation ; from
this time he was entirely admitted into the secrets
of the mystery of the incarnation, for when he
learned it from the angel he was ready to give up
all selfish feelings. He became at once the foster-
father of Our Lord : he was the representative of
God the Father, who in communicating to him the
honor of paternity to the incarnate Word willed
that he should call Him by the name of son, a name
which He alone gives in heaven to the uncreate
Word. Thus God who formerly had said He would
give His glory to no one, now, as an exceptional
favor, communicates in a manner to a mortal that
paternity which is the glory of the eternal Father.
What is still more, God, according to St. Bernard,
in giving to Joseph the name of father, gave him
also a father's heart, that is, the authority, the
solicitude, and the love of a father.

Joseph was also the representative of the Holy

Ghost, who confided to him the Virgin Mary, placing His spouse under Joseph's protection and direction. The Father and the Holy Ghost intrust to him what is most dear to them. To what sublimity of virtue must he have attained to acquit himself worthily of such a charge! And Mary on her part gave Joseph her heart and love and faithful attachment. Never did a wife love her husband so tenderly, so ardently, nor revere him more profoundly. Mary and Joseph were but one heart and soul: they were of the same mind, same affection, and each of them was the other's second self. The heart of Mary with that of Joseph and the heart of Joseph with that of Mary—who ever could imagine a union so intimate, and graces so great! From that time forward St. Joseph deserves the many titles of respect which the piety of the people gives him.

The Birth of St. John.

In course of time Elizabeth gave birth to the child; the wonders of God were not yet completed in the case of this great favorite of God. Wonderful events happened at the birth of this child which we shall relate. In this chapter, my dear children, we shall treat also of the youth and childhood of the precursor of Christ; it stands so well beside the childhood of Jesus. St. John was therefore also the precursor of Our Lord in the beauty of his life.

On the eighth day the child was to be circumcised and a name was to be given to him. The neighbors and relations, as was customary, gathered about to proclaim the mercy of God and to make arrangements for the ceremony. They began to speculate as to the probable name of this child : one suggested a name because the grandfather had borne it ; a second proposed another name because a rich and influential uncle was so called ; some thought he should be named after

his father, Zachary ; but Elizabeth, divinely inspired, insisted that he should be called *John.*
Zachary had not spoken since the days of the appearance of the angel in the Temple, and could
not speak. So he made signs for a writing-tablet,
and clearly wrote on it, " John is his name." At
that moment his speech returned to him ; it was
like a great effort. With a cry of exultation he felt
his tongue loosed and he spoke aloud in thanksgiving to the Lord. The news of these wonderful
manifestations spread over all that country : people remembered what had happened in the Temple
and they said among themselves, " What think you
shall this boy be one day ? the hand of the Lord is
evidently upon him." But Zachary was filled with
the Spirit of God : his mind saw into the future,
he saw the Messias and the salvation which was
to come from Him, and broke out into these words
of the " Benedictus " :

" Blessed be the Lord, the God of Israel, because
He hath looked down upon His people and hath
wrought their redemption.

" He hath raised up in the house of David His
son, an invincible power to be our salvation.

" According to that which He hath promised us
by the mouth of the holy prophets, from the beginning of time.

"A salvation whereby He will preserve us, for the accomplishment of His loving-kindness unto our fathers.

" And as a remembrance of His holy covenant the oath which He swore to Abraham, our father.

" So that delivered from the hand of our enemies and freed from fear we may worship Him.

" In righteousness and holiness in His sight even all the days of our life.

"And thou, child, shall be called the prophet of the Most High.

" Thou shalt walk before the Lord to prepare His way.

" To declare unto His people salvation in the pardon of their sins.

" Pardon through the bowels of the mercy of Our Lord.

"Whereby a star, rising to the heights of heaven, hath visited us.

" Illumining them that sit in the shadow and darkness of death."

St. John grew up under the tender care of his mother to a certain age ; while still very young his heart inclined to solitude and to prayer. The Spirit of the Lord was upon him and he did not relish the things of this world nor even the innocent play of children. He found the retreat which

he so much coveted in the desert near-by; thither
he betook himself at an early age. In that hilly,
barren country he must have found a convenient
cave for protection at night, and to a certain extent from the inclemency of the winter; here he
lived alone, praying and fasting. He was preparing himself for the mission which God intended
for him and which he had made up his mind to
fulfil to the best of his ability. St. Luke says of
him, " The child grew and was strengthened in
spirit: and was in the deserts until the day of
his manifestation to Israel."

St. John first of all practised a most penitential
life. St. Matthew describes him as wearing a garment made of camel's-hair, a leather girdle about
his loins, and his food of locusts and wild honey,
and whatever food that was clean, according to the
Jewish law; his bed was the hard ground: and
with extraordinary hardihood he suffered the cold
and the heat of that rugged climate. This he un-
derwent willingly, not for any sins, for he was
sanctified before he was born, but in order to conquer the flesh and preserve himself from every
stain of sin. Hence Our Lord praised St. John,
saying: " What went you out into the desert to
see? a reed shaken with the wind? But what
went you out to see? a man clothed in soft gar-

ments ? Behold they that are clothed in soft garments are in the houses of kings. But what went you out to see ? a prophet ? Yea, I tell you, and more than a prophet, for this is he of whom it is written : Behold I send My angel before Thy face who shall prepare Thy way before Thee."

St. John was constantly engaged in contemplation and prayer : he was not roving about like a wild man of the solitudes, but he was led by the Spirit into solitude there to speak to his heart. And certainly God favored His angel with many consolations, and made amends to him for all that he had given up: riches, honors, dignities, the delights of the paternal roof. He had chosen the better part and persevered in it. He was also of a strong mind. No doubt almighty God frequently allowed temptations to come to him : the devil pictured to him the loss of his parents, the comfort of a home, but he remained where he was, knowing that this was the will of God. He cultivated purity of soul and body, as we are told that he " grew and was strengthened in spirit." We read in the Psalms : " Blessed is the man whose help is from Thee ; in his heart he hath disposed to ascend by steps ; " that he went " from virtue to virtue : the God of gods shall be seen in Sion." He grew " as a shining light that goeth

forwards and increaseth even to perfect day." No
wonder then that John the Baptist became so great
in the service of God !

My dear children, if you, too, would become
good and persevering in the work of your salvation and that of others, you must begin early, in
fact endeavor to preserve your baptismal innocence
through life, so that you may always be an object
of the love of God.

The Nativity of Our Lord.

NAZARETH, which was to be the blessed abode of
Jesus for many years, was not to be His birthplace.
A little while before His birth an edict of Cæsar
Augustus was sent out to all the Jews living in
Palestine that they must be enrolled in order to
make a census, and that they must go to the city
to which they belonged. The whole Roman Empire was to be counted, so that it might be seen
at a glance how many soldiers were under arms,
how many citizens employed in peaceful pursuits,
what was the size of the available fleet, what reve-
nues were to be derived from the kingdoms and
provinces, an estimate of the expenses, and a cal-
culation of the income. Peace reigned throughout
the world, the warlike gate of the Temple of Janus
was closed, the great Roman Empire dominated
over every known land and held sway over every
sea. It was just the time when the Prince of
peace should enter this world. So then, to inscribe
himself, Joseph quitted his beloved and quiet city

of Nazareth. It took four days' travel by foot to
reach Bethlehem. Joseph and Mary travelled
slowly on account of Mary's condition : the journey was probably made easier for her by riding a
donkey. St. Joseph, carrying a staff, walked beside the Virgin holding the guide straps of the
donkey. They passed outside of the walls of Jerusalem, on their left were the walls of Mount Sion ;
they passed the lower pool of Gihon, up the hill
of Evil Counsel, until they reached the plain of
Rephaim, and then turned to the road to Bethlehem. Now and then, as they journeyed on, Joseph
related some incident of the struggles with the
Philistines on that plain, he pointed out Rachel's
tomb which Abraham had bought for a family
burying-place, and often as he raised his compas-
sionate eyes to her face he saw there the ecstatic
beauty of one engaged in prayer. The crowds were
becoming more dense, every one striving to get to
Bethlehem by a certain time.

In the distance they could now already discern
the ancient city to which they were hastening.
The village is located on a long whitish range of
hills, the slopes covered with olive and fig trees,
and vines growing along arbor-like trestles as if
shade were looked for more than fruit. It was
towards evening when they arrived at Bethlehem:

they wandered from house to house, but there was
no room, so they had to look for humbler dwell-
ings. They called at one of the khans, which at
ordinary times afforded shelter for man and beast,
but on this occasion the travel to Bethlehem was
so great that even these places were crowded. A
khan was no luxurious hotel or hostelry; it was
a simple stone enclosure, the height of a man,
within which merchandise could be stored for a
time. Sheds for cattle were all that were to be
found there. It was something of the nature of a
village green, where the markets are held and business of all kinds is transacted. The stranger that
came along looked for no house. He spread a
blanket on the ground near his goods and beasts,
and there lay down to take his rest. He brought
with him his own food and fodder for his animals.
Such was the aspect of the place before which
Joseph and Mary presented themselves. As Joseph came nearer, the painful certainty broke on
him that it would be almost impossible to find
shelter. Every place was occupied. Within and
without was a clamorous, pushing multitude, all
looking for a resting-place.

Then said Joseph to Mary: "It is as I feared,
my beloved one, there is no room for us anywhere.
I will try to reach the gatekeeper; perhaps he

will do me a favor. He may have some place in
reserve." When Joseph reached the keeper, he
said to him : " Peace of Jehovah be with you. I
am a Bethlehemite. Is there no room to be found
for one in distress ? " The keeper, already grown
impatient, turned an angry glance on him and
said : " There is no more room, as you can see for
yourself." " Ah ! but have pity on her whom I
am conducting to Bethlehem. She is my wife.
The night is cold, and she will die if left in the
open air. She is the daughter of Joachim and
Ann of this place ; but they are dead." " I knew
them," was the answer. " They were good and
pious people."

" We, too," continued Joseph, pleading, " are of
the royal house of David."

There was no greater boast on the lips of a
Jew than to be of the royal house of David. It
was a family ever held in greatest respect. Though
a thousand years had passed, still the intimate connection of that king with the sacred writings of
the Jews kept their love for the family alive.

The keeper then said : " I cannot turn you
away. I will conduct you to a place of refuge."

" My blessing on you, my dear friend," said Joseph ; " may Jehovah shower upon you His greatest favors for this kindness." Then Joseph sought

Mary, and the keeper, taking hold of the leading
straps of the animal, led the way. They walked
through the crowds of men and beasts, some of
them sleeping and others guarding their merchandise. They descended the slope, and the keeper
guided them to a structure partially built against
the side of a hill ; but so narrow was it that you
were sure it must hide the face of a cave, and so
it did. " Here," said the keeper, " is shelter which
I can let you have. This cave must have been a
resort of your ancestor David. From the field below us and from the well down in the valley he
used to drive his flocks here for safety." And con-
tentedly Mary and Joseph came to it to take possession. To the Jew of that period there was nothing revolting in making a temporary home in a
cave, and Bethlehem especially abounded in caves.
When looking for shelter these herdsmen knew
how to be satisfied ; the shepherd did not want
anything better than this.

The keeper drew a wooden bolt that barred the
door and swung open the gate that led to the cave,
and invited them to enter. The guests entered.
The darkness was so great that even with the help
of the lamps they were unable for a while to ob-
serve anything. At last they could see a floor,
smooth and well beaten but dusty; piles of grain and

fodder in a corner, earthenware and old crockery in the centre. Mangers of wood were ranged along the walls for sheep, spider-webs tangled and torn hung like rags in dusty festoons from the ceiling.

" You are welcome; what you find here you may make use of," said the keeper. Joseph at once busied himself in setting things in order. Suddenly the cave was lighted up with a bright light from heaven, which continued as long as the Holy Family dwelt there. Everything else was now in darkness, and in the silence of the night men and beasts slept.

With a heart full of compassion St. Joseph had done all he could to make the surroundings more comfortable. He knew now that this was the place where the King of kings, the Saviour of mankind, was to make His appearance in the world. Picture to yourself Mary on her knees in the humble attitude of prayer, absorbed in the contemplation of the mercies of God. Not far away is Joseph filled with the love of God, and longing to be of use in this trial. He would rather that Jesus should be born in a house, for he sees the discomforts of the place they then were in ; but he is resigned to the will of God in all things. How happy would Mary and Joseph have been had they remained in their humble dwelling in Naza-

reth! but so it had been preordained by divine
Providence. But the blissful moment has come!

At midnight a watchman of the khan cried out
to some sleepers: "Hey there! here is something
extraordinary. What light is that in the sky?"
The people saw the rays of a singularly bright
star descending and spreading out over a good portion of the plain, and there, distinctly lighted up
by the illumination, could be seen the flocks and
the shepherds. Nature seemed to be at peace;
solemn stillness reigned everywhere. The world
appeared to stand still, waiting for a great event
to take place. Suddenly the adorable Child appeared surrounded by a bright light, and with eyes
full of love He stretched out His tiny hands to His
Mother. She took Him into her arms and adored
Him, the Creator and Saviour of the world. Mary
was now the Mother of God. Hers was an unspeakable happiness. She had preserved her virginity
in giving birth to this divine Child. As St. Augustine says, she was a virgin before His birth, during
His birth, and after His birth.

Mary hastened to wrap the child in swaddling-
clothes: the night was chilly, and the divine Infant was exposed to the cold in this cave un-
suited for human habitation. That Child, though
the God-man, had subjected Himself to all the

vicissitudes of life, and like other babes He felt the severe cold of those mountains of Judea. No doubt also the first cry escaped from the divine Infant and the first tears coursed down His cheeks.

There was no cradle there, nor bed, only dusty mangers, made of wood rudely put together by the shepherds who sometimes came there. Putting some straw within one of these and spreading a little linen cloth over it, Mary laid the Child on this humble bed. Then it was that St. Joseph also knelt in adoration of the holy Child and poured forth his soul in silent prayer. We feel certain, too, that he was often privileged to take the Child Jesus in his arms, and then, no doubt, he showed signs of greatest tenderness and love not only as a father, but as one who was persuaded of the divine character of the Child. With faith no less than that of the shepherds, with an enthusiasm as great as that of the Magi, he made that public act of faith by which he openly acknowledged the presence among men of the Son of God.

Unite, my dear children, in the adoration and love of our blessed Lady and St. Joseph at the manger. Go before the altar of the Blessed Sacrament ; the Child Jesus is there as He was in the

cave of Bethlehem. From His tabernacle He
blesses you, He watches you, and loves you as He
did on this first Christmas morning in the stable
at Bethlehem.

The Adoration of the Shepherds.

Down in the valley, perhaps a mile distant, were shepherds with their flocks. To protect the sheep from the marauding wolf they were driven at night into enclosures surrounded by walls as high as a man, and were all secure. Near the gate of the sheepfold the shepherds kindled a fire; some were talking and others were stretched at full length on their sheepskins. They usually went bareheaded, their hair stood up straight and unkempt, thick beards covered their chins and throats, mantles of the skins of kids and lambs wrapped them from neck to knee, leaving their arms exposed. Leather belts secured these rude garments to their bodies. From their shoulders hung a leather bag for food, and coarse sandals protected their feet. You would say they were a rough set of men, illiterate and almost savage; still they must have been deeply religious, tender-hearted too; but they led a very primitive life, constantly wandering about, either herding their own sheep or the flocks of some rich farmer that were entrusted to their care.

But these men, rude and simple as they were, had some education. On the Sabbath day they performed their purifications, as other Jews were accustomed to do, and assembled in the synagogues. They listened to the reading of the sacred Scriptures, and often heard that the Lord was one God, and that they must love Him with all their soul. Certainly those who were to find favor in His sight must have been noted for the love of God, and were now to be rewarded by the privilege of which we are about to speak. These shepherds were keeping their night watches, when at midnight they sprang to their feet alarmed and dazzled; fear grasped their very hearts. "What is this?" they gasped rather than spoke. The sky looked as if it were afire, but there was one particular place that claimed their attention. A bright spot in all this light, growing more and more distinct, seemed to approach until it assumed the form of a man. Bright shining wings extended upwards from his shoulders in graceful lines. He was dressed in garments glittering with gold and soft as finest silk. With a countenance radiant with joy and with a calm smile, he bade the shepherds take courage. "Fear not," he said, "I am an angel from God.

Behold, I bring you good tidings of great joy, which shall be to all the people." Assured by these words and by the peace of God which entered their souls, they no longer feared. They understood at once that there was news of the Messias. The long-expected Child is at last born. "For this day," continued the angel, "is born to you a Saviour, who is Christ the Lord, in the city of David." But there must be a sign by which this great divine Visitor could be known. Where should they find the Infant? In a palace, in the houses of the great? They knew that such people as they were would not find welcome or entrance there.

To this day the Jews are looking for a Messias. But what notions have they of His appearance? He is to be a great leader; fear and trembling will strike His adversaries. They will flee and leave to the Jews the land of promise—the land flowing with milk and honey. The shepherds were Jews, and perhaps they, too, had notions of this kind; but the sign is given them. "This shall be a sign to you," said the angel. "You shall find the Infant wrapped in swaddling-clothes, and laid in a manger." The shepherds were not astonished at this strange message, but were happy in the thought that they were to see the great Messias. Then the angel ascended from the earth, radiant with light, and as he soared high into the air a countless multitude of angelic spirits gathered about him, and all sang in one full chorus, " Glory to God in the highest and on earth peace to men of good will." The hills re-echoed the glorious canticle again and again. It was repeated through every variety of melody until it died away in the great vaults of heaven.

This was the great manifestation that God gave His divine Son when He appeared in human form for the first time on this earth. He called the angels down from heaven to adore Him. As it is written in the sacred Scriptures, " All the angels shall adore Him." In astonishment the shepherds looked at one another and asked : " Who was that great, bright angel ? " " It must have been Gabriel, the Lord's messenger." " What did he say ? " " He said that Christ is born." " But where shall we find Him ? Where is He born ? The angel did not tell us where to look. He said we would find the Infant wrapped in swaddling-clothes and laid in a manger. Why, it must be that He is to be found where the mangers are. That place we know well. We have often seen the cave and have passed stormy nights there. Let us go thither and search for Him; it is not far away."

They set out together, taking with them some

tender lambs as offerings to the Holy Family.
When they arrived at the gate of the inn, and were
making their way to the rear, the keeper stopped
them and asked, "What do you want?" They
answered: "We have seen a great wonder, and
probably you, too, have seen that great light over
yonder. An angel spoke to us words of joy that
a Christ is born to the world. Allow us to pro-
ceed then, for they are in the cave beyond, where
the mangers are. We are told to look for Him
there. Come with us and let us visit the Child."
Having arrived at the cave they found Joseph.
They asked with anxiety: "Where is the Child
that is born this night, the Christ? for we have
seen His angel and he directed us hither." St.
Joseph answered quietly, "The Child is here with
His Mother." Respectfully they entered, and with
eager eyes they searched for the new-born Babe,
and found Him lying on a little straw in a
manger. The Child made no outward sign of intelligence or recognition, but like other infants it
was closely wrapped in swaddling-clothes and slept.
"It is the Lord. Yes, this is the Babe of which
we were told by heavenly messengers." They
formed a close circle around the Mother and Child,
and falling on their knees they kissed the hem of
the Mother's garment. Then they related all that

had happened to the wondering Mother and Joseph, who listened attentively and thought of God's mercy to man.

Then the shepherds went back to their flocks and told the story to their companions who had been left behind. The little city in which all these wonders took place was ignorant of God's great mercy to the human race. Bethlehem was not considered worthy of the grace of knowing that the Saviour was born.

O, Mother of Jesus, how great was thy love for thy divine Son! Such was the unspeakable magnificence of her soul in that love and first adoration, that the praises of all the saints and angels could not equal hers.

What graces were poured out on Joseph that he, too, might worthily adore the Lord! He is the foster-father of Jesus; he is a vessel of divine predilection, eternally predestined to the great and singular office of being the protector of the divine Infant and His Mother. "Jesus is born to us. Let us go and adore Him," sings the Church, and she leads us all to the crib of Bethlehem. With fond delight she shows us the surroundings. There is the weeping Infant in swaddling-clothes and laid in a manger; there is St. Joseph caring for the divine Infant; there is the

Mother Mary full of love and adoration for the Child ; near the manger is an ox and an ass. That Child is God, that Mother is our dear heavenly Queen, that Joseph is our dear patron. We too belong to that family even at this distant time, for we too love Jesus, Mary, and Joseph.

Dear children, let us go in spirit to Bethlehem and learn the things the shepherds learned ; practise the same virtues of faith and humility which they practised. Let us be as generous as they were in their poverty. Let us approach with their eyes of faith and see all that is to be seen. There is the little Babe of Bethlehem looking at us with a sweet smile, His arms extended towards us in mercy and kindness. This is the great God who shall save His people of Israel ; He is the eternal God, all-powerful and infinite, who in heaven at God's right hand holds the universe in the palm of His hand ; who has created all that you see about you ; who has created you too. Without Him nothing can exist in the whole world. To know that God created all things is easy to profess, but to recognize the omnipotent God in this Child is a stumbling-block to many.

Assisted by the grace of God and enlightened by His wisdom we shall not hesitate ; but like the shepherds, falling down with love, reverence, and adoration before the God made man, we will offer Him our homage.

Whom do you see most frequently in our churches at the crib admiring the sweet Infant? Little children. Grown people are sometimes moved to tears as they gaze on the little flock, trooping up hand in hand, making their quaint genuflections and moving their lips in prayer; or when a mother with her child kneels before the altar and tells her little one the story of Bethlehem, and asks the child to make the sacrifice of its penny to the Infant Jesus.

My dear children, be as familiar with the Child Jesus as you are with other children, for in this devotion the divine Child speaks especially to children. How full of awe you would be if you should see God in all His majesty! Then you might fear and tremble, but the love of the Christ-Child is a kind of divine worship, of which neither angels nor men ever could have dreamed. And this Child is so small, so kind, that the most appropriate offering to Him is the love and familiarity of children.

Coleridge in an admirable stanza describes the finding of the Child by the shepherds:

> The shepherds went their hasty way,
> And found the lonely stable-shed

Wherein the Virgin Mother lay:
  And now they checked their eager tread,
For to the Babe that at her bosom clung,
  A mother's song the Virgin Mother sung.
They told her how a glorious light,
  Streaming from a heavenly throng,
Around them shone, suspended night,
  While sweeter than a mother's song
Blest angels heralded the Saviour's birth,
  Glory to God on high! and peace on earth.

The ox and the ass are always represented in pictures of the stable of Bethlehem. Probably they are found there because it is a stable, and naturally enough some such animals may have been there. Perhaps, too, it is in consequence of the old prophecy of Isaias : " The ox knoweth his owner and the ass his master's crib." Their presence does not seem incongruous, because all nature adored its Infant Lord. The good Breton peasants believe that at midnight on Christmas the ox and the ass are gifted with speech, and so they hide themselves in the stable to listen to the conversation which these animals are supposed to hold among themselves.

As the shepherds joyfully left their flocks at the dead of night to look for the new-born Babe, so we, faithful children of God and His Church, will gladly gather round the altar at the invita-

tion of the priests, for they are God's messengers
and angels. Our faith teaches us that there is the
same Jesus, under the appearance of bread, in the
Blessed Sacrament. The shepherds saw a little
Child and they adored Him. We see only the
consecrated bread, but we know that Jesus is
there, and we also adore Him.

What great blessings did not the shepherds de-
rive from that visit to Our Lord ? Mary held the
divine Infant out towards them and blessed them.
Pray to these happy men in heaven, that we, too,
after having faithfully followed the Lord, may
one day also enjoy a joyous Christmas in heaven.

The Magi.

OUR good Lord, the Saviour of all men, rich and poor, had called the humble and ignorant shepherds to His sacred crib. He loves the poor because they have by necessity the virtues which naturally endear them to His heart. To the poor He preached, and those who came into close contact with Him were also poor. The first He admitted to adore Him were poor Jews. Now He wishes to have the Gentiles come to Him, men of learning, wealth, and public standing. By a miracle He called the Magi from the East. He brought them by the light of a star to the very cave in Bethlehem.

It is quite certain that there were other nations that expected the coming of the Messias. Some, perhaps all, had vague prophecies among them concerning Him. Even among the barbarous but poetic tribes of the Norseman distinct mention is made of the coming of the Expected of nations.

The Jews had clear promises of the coming of

the Messias, and the other nations who had read
the sacred books of the Jews also learned from
these prophecies that a Saviour was to be born.

When the Israelites on their way to the Promised Land were about to pass through the country
of Moab, King Balac summoned to his court a
heathen prophet named Balaam to curse the Hebrew people; but the Lord compelled the false
prophet against his will to pronounce a blessing.
So looking far away into the future ages, and
raising his voice he said: "A star shall rise out
of Jacob, and a sceptre shall spring up from Israel and shall strike the chiefs of Moab, and shall
waste all the children of Seth. And He shall possess Idumea; the inheritance of Seir shall come
to their enemies, but Israel shall do manfully.
Out of Jacob shall He come that shall rule and
shall destroy the remains of the city." This is
a remarkable prophecy. It clearly shows that a
Messias shall come, that a star shall appear, and
that the nations of the East shall be brought to
the Lord.

The heathen nations had come to believe that
among the Jews a mighty king would one day be
born, who would bring the Gentiles and their
whole country under Jewish dominion. In the
course of long ages people naturally lost sight of

these wonderful prophecies; still the tradition always remained, especially in the East, where men were very studious in religious matters and in astronomy. Years upon years passed. Wise men hoped that in their day the star would appear; but like the long wait which the human race had gone through, so also these wise men were doomed to a long expectation. Generations after generations died, still the hope of the coming of a Redeemer did not die with them. The watchers on the tower waiting for the star were replaced from age to age by others.

The Magi were pious and wise people; they appear at all times to have worshipped one supreme divinity. In those Eastern countries there were neither altars nor statues in the temples. The choirs never marched with other than reverent gravity, sending up to God their solemn chants and prayers.

The religion of the Persians spread along into Mesopotamia, and thus it came under the influence of the captives from Jerusalem. Daniel, the prophet, was certainly well known in the vicinity of his captivity. We know from Scripture that this prophet, after his introduction into the palace of Nabuchodonosor, showed himself more wise than the soothsayers of Chaldea, and hence through the favor of the prince he was placed at their head. Under the succeeding dynasties his fame increased, and was afterwards confirmed by the triumphs of the Persians.

The Magi were from the same country, and could not have been ignorant of the predictions of Daniel concerning the coming of the Messias, in which he had gone even so far as to mark the year, month, and hour of the Redeemer's birth. From Daniel they had learned that the Saint of saints, who should receive the divine anointment, was that very One whom Balaam had beheld rising from Israel like a star.

From the Magi the prophecies were disseminated among the people, and at this time there was a settled conviction that a king was to arise from Judea who should conquer the world, and with great longing they expected his coming.

You cannot, my dear children, form an idea of the hardships that human beings had to undergo in those remote times. The condition of the common people was mostly slavery. Men had to suffer all the privations of war and want. They did not have the conveniences of the present day. Comforts were very few ; houses were mere huts. Was it a wonder, then, that all humanity sighed for a Redeemer from this heavy load ? Would it not be reasonable to think that the One who was to free men from the slavery of Satan and sin would also better their condition in every other way ? The advent of Christ has done a great deal towards the alleviation of human misery. The world has become more enlightened, the condition of woman has improved, arts and sciences flourish among the nations of the world, and all men have felt the wonderful effects of His coming.

The Magi knew what the nations expected and on what foundations they trusted. They were Gentiles whom God called to be added to the chosen race of His people on earth. A new era of mercy and goodness was to be inaugurated by the admission of these men to the adoration of the true God.

My dear children, as these wise men were studying the heavens a new star appeared, and as they were gazing at it, it took the form of a child and beckoned them to follow.

> A star, not seen before, in heaven appearing,
> Guided the Wise Men thither from the East
> To honor Thee with incense, myrrh, and gold.
> By whose bright course, led on, they found the place.
> Affirming at Thy star new graven in heaven
> By which they knew the King of Israel born.*

---

* Milton's *Paradise Regained.*

A tradition asserts that these Magi were the representatives of three great nations who descended from Noe's sons. Starting from different points and following the guiding star, the Magi travelled unknown to one another until they met on the way and found they were on the same errand. Each had been guided by a star, but at their meeting the stars united and became one. Then they told one another their reasons for taking this journey. The Greek told his story first. " I believed in God invisible, yet supreme. I also believed it possible so to yearn for His coming with all my soul, that He would take compassion and give me answer. From a poor Jewish slave I heard of the true God, the Lawmaker of their people. One night in my dreams I saw a star beginning to burn. Slowly it rose, and, drawing near, it stood above my door so that its light shone full upon me. Then a voice said, 'O Gaspar, blessed art thou ! With these two others who come from the uttermost parts of the earth thou shalt see Him that is promised. In the morning arise and go forth to meet Him.' When I awoke I remembered my vision. I looked for the star, and truly it was a reality. I followed it, and here we have met."

Melchior had also his story to tell. " I studied

the ancient system of religion in the East, following God through all stages and becoming one with
Him, and with the desire to know more of Him fill-
ing my heart. To me also in a dream came a vision,
saying ' Thy love has conquered ; the redemption
is at hand. With others from different quarters
of the earth come and see the new-born God.'
And there appeared a star which showed me the
way and has never deserted me. Through all
these deserts this thought was always uppermost
in my mind : I am to see the Redeemer, to speak
to Him, to worship Him."

Now it was Balthassar's turn to give an account
of the manner in which he had been led by the
star. Egypt was a country of very great learning.
Probably no other people were as learned as the
Egyptians. The children of Israel for a long time
had been in bondage in Egypt. From them
came the knowledge of the coming of the Messias.
" One night," said Balthassar, " a light suddenly
appeared, and soon I saw a star rising which
moved towards me, and I heard the words,
' Blessed art thou. Arise, thy redemption is at
hand.' I arose and followed the guiding light
which brought me here."

The Magi journeyed on, each one relating his
experience of God's mercy to him, until they

reached Jerusalem, when the star disappeared.
They therefore knew they were at their journey's
end, and, entering the city, they made their way
to the royal palace and asked of the curious multitude the extraordinary question, "Where is the
new-born King of the Jews? We have seen His
star in the East, and have come to adore Him."
But no one knew. They inquired of Herod, but
he had not heard of the great event of which these
men spoke.

The Magi came to Jerusalem under the guid-
ance of the star. Up to this it had shone beauti-
fully and brightly, but at the gates of the royal
city its light was extinguished, as if the Magi were
at their journey's end. But they were forced to
enter the city to make inquiry. They went to the
royal palace thinking that there they would most
probably find what they sought. The city
was dark and quiet; there seemed to be no rejoicing there; it did not look as if Jerusalem was
rejoicing over the birth of a new-born king.
There is usually great feasting at the birth of a
new-born aspirant to the throne, but here everything was silent and showed no sign of any extraordinary event. The Magi sent their servants
in advance to ask, "Where is the new-born King?
we have come from the East to adore Him."

What consternation this caused among the peaceful inhabitants ! They feared a bloody revolution; they knew what it meant to them if they showed signs of joy at the news ; for Herod was not very firmly seated on his throne, and were he to hear of any demonstration of joy he would send his soldiers into the city and the inhabitants would be struck down by the sword. Cases of this kind had taken place on several occasions, and though the people sighed for a change of rulers they were careful not to show it.

The question of the Magi flew from lip to lip and soon reached Herod's ears. He, too, was thrown into alarm, for he knew the mind of the people, and the question did not forebode any good; it was like the muttering of a distant threat that his days of supremacy were at an end. It was known that this new-born Babe was destined to be the new occupant of the throne, the new-born King of the Jews : it was easy to see from the excitement which suddenly pervaded the city that all Jerusalem interpreted the inquiry of the Magi in that same light.

Picture to yourself the consternation of the people and their ruler when a foreign embassy actually invaded their city looking for a new-born king. Herod did not say that these men were deluded. He had an idea that it was the Messias that was in question, so he called the scribes together and laid before them this momentous question, "Where is the new-born King of the Jews?" The Magi concluded that Bethlehem was the place in which the Messias was to be born, for they found in the old prophecies a distinct announcement in these words: "And thou, O Bethlehem, the land of Juda, art not the least among the princes of Juda. For out of thee shall come forth the Captain who is to rule My people Israel." Herod also came to the same conclusion, and he said to the Wise Men: "Go and diligently inquire after the Child, and when you have found Him, bring me word again, that I, also, may come and adore Him." In this manner Herod dismissed the Magi, who at once set about their search with which they were commissioned by the king himself. A servant of Herod preceded them and showed them the way to the Joppe gate. They encouragingly said to one another: "Let us go on to Bethlehem as the king advised, and not tarry on the way. We can rest when our mission is over." At the gate directions were given them by the attendants, and they set out on their journey. Everything was dark and they almost despaired. Had their star deserted them? Was it no longer to guide them, since they knew now where they had to go? But soon their trouble was changed into joy. All at once there was a bright flash that illumined the whole country about. The Magi were almost blinded by the brightness that shone so suddenly in the darkness, but when their eyes became accustomed to the light they recognized their familiar star, which beckoned them to follow. They shouted a joyful salute to their heavenly guide, saying: " Let us on. God is with us! God is with us!" They travelled on securely, firmly, and quietly, needing no further directions.

It was towards morning that the Magi approached Bethlehem, the star moving on before them, its brilliancy brightening up the road and the trees on the wayside. Those who saw the light were awe-stricken. They thought it was a slowly passing meteor. It approached the khan, shedding its brightness over the enclosure, and then remained stationary at the cave. The caravan entered the gate, to the astonishment of the keeper. He looked with wonder at the camels of unusual size and whiteness, which moved with such stateliness. The star revealed the rich trappings of the animals and the wealth which they carried in packs. He saw the owners seated under their canopies, while little bells were making an unusual tinkle as they moved slowly on, intent on the light before them. In the strange light the animals looked like a vision, and the keeper was so struck with terror that he did not hear the salute of the travellers until it was repeated. "Is this Bethlehem of Juda?" "Yes," he said. "The town itself, however, lies a short distance farther on." "We have followed," the Magi said, "this star which you see, and now it stands motionless over there before a house. Is the newborn King of the Jews here? Was a child born here?" And the keeper answered: "In that house which covers the entrance to a cave a child was recently born. On the night on which it was born a bright light, something like this, illumined the whole country. It must be that Child for whom you are looking." "Yes, surely," the Magi answered, "that is certainly the Child. Make haste; let us adore Him." Then, as if to tell the Magi that they had truly found what they were looking for, the star rose higher and higher in the heavens, to show that it was withdrawn by divine hands, until at last it was lost among the other stars in the firmament.

The souls of the Magi were filled with a heavenly joy, as they crowded to the door and entered the rude place. They saw the Child, and close by the Mother. With hearts overflowing with love they asked, "Is this the Child ?" and Mary replied, "Yes." She took the Child in her arms, and, sitting down, presented Our Lord to them ; and they fell down and adored Him. The Child was as other children. There was no sign of divinity about Him. He spoke not, though prayers, adorations, and supplications were poured out at His feet. But the Wise Men of the East did not for an instant think that they had been deceived, that they must look for another Child greater, more divine-looking than this one. No, they believed and adored. Their faith rested upon signs sent them by Him whom we know as the Father ; God the Creator who had worked all these miracles, and had sent the star to lead the Wise Men to the feet of the Infant God.

Tradition tells us that the three Magi represent the three stages of manhood. Gaspar is pictured as a very old man with long white hair and long white beard, with the features of a descendant of Japhet, the European patriarch. Balthassar belongs to the Semitic race ; he is middle-aged and black-haired. Melchior is the youngest ; he is represented as a negro or Moor with little black pages in attendance.

When the Magi appeared before Our Lord, they
fell at full length before the Child, and adored
Him as their King and Saviour. They had
brought with them offerings for the new-born
King, so that the prophecy might be fulfilled:
" The kings of Tarshish and the islands shall offer
presents ; the kings of the Arabians and of Saba
shall bring gifts." They offered incense, the em-
blem of prayer, as to a god. They gave Him gold,
the token of His royalty, and myrrh as to the Saviour, who by His death would redeem the world.
Some say that each king offered gold as a tribute
of subjects to their Monarch. Mary received these
gifts, in the name of her Son, and then gave the
gold to the poor of the neighborhood.

In return for the gold, incense, and myrrh the
Lord gave the Magi the spiritual blessings of love,
meekness, and perfect faith.

> The Magi of the East, in sandals worn,
> Knelt reverent, sweeping round
> With long white beards, their gifts upon the ground;
> The incense, myrrh, and gold
> These baby hands were impotent to hold.*

We are also told that the Magi made presents
to Mary and Joseph.

* Browning.

The Wise Men remained for some time in Bethlehem. They could not tear themselves away from the presence of their Saviour. At the foot of the manger they received the new faith from the Infant Jesus, and listened to many explanations from Mary and Joseph.

In vain did Herod await the coming of the Wise Men to give him a report of their success in finding the new-born Babe, for an angel had come to them in their sleep and told them not to return to Herod, so they returned home by another way.

The Magi had learned the lesson of self-abnegation and poverty from Our Lord. They gave all their possessions to the poor ; they laid aside their rich robes and went about preaching the birth of the Infant God. They were baptized, and fully instructed in the Christian religion, and became the first missionaries to their people in the East. Full of zeal for their Master, whom they had seen an Infant at His Mother's bosom, they preached Christ, and eventually died martyrs to their faith. The Empress St. Helena discovered their remains long after, and brought these precious relics to Constantinople. Some time later they were transferred to the cathedral at Cologne, where they now rest in a magnificent tomb. The shrine of the three kings is well known throughout

Europe, and from all quarters the devout gather there to witness the exposition of the relics.

Jesus is the King of kings, the Teacher of the learnèd, the Master of heaven and earth. Everything above and below is His, because He has created all. Kings obey and adore Him. Philosophers and wise men should take Jesus for their model, and follow His sacred teaching. All the wealth and power of the earth should be offered to Him, for in reality all belongs to Him.

O little Infant Jesus, how great Thou art! Our blessed Lady holds Thee in her hands, and yet Thou art more immense than the world, more powerful than kings, wiser than all philosophers and doctors. Thou hast nothing, not even a little bed, and yet Thou art richer than all the wealth of the world. Make me understand the honor that it is for me to be Thy faithful little servant; to bow down before Thee, so that Thou mayst raise me to a throne in heaven.

The Circumcision.

WHETHER Our Lord was presented in the Temple before the coming of the Magi matters little; the time of the arrival of the Magi is not stated, but the circumcision always took place eight days after the birth of a male child. In this chapter we ought to note three events. First, the circumcision, by which a sign was made on the body; then, a name was given to the child; and lastly, he was presented to God as the first-born.

Although not subject to the law, because He was God who made it, still Our Lord wished to be circumcised. It was an act of humiliation, it acknowledged the fact that He was outside the family of God and by this ceremony was introduced into it. This law was given to Abraham that he might set it as a sign on all his spiritual family; but Jesus wished to submit to the pain for our salvation and as an example of humility, obedience, and patience. This ceremony need not be performed in the Temple or synagogue; when the child was eight days old it might be circumcised by some respectable relative. Perhaps St.

Joseph shed the first blood of Our Lord, and it seems only right that he should be the head of the family, the natural priest of the family of God. The time had now come to give the Child a name. This name had been given by God the Father, and had been repeated by the angel to Mary. He was to be called Jesus, a name that spoke of salvation to the Jews. The sublimest titles of Christ are the Messias, the Majesty of the Son of God, the Anointed, the great King, the Pontiff; by these names He was known in the Old Testament. He is the High Priest of God in the midst of His creatures, the supreme King of men and angels; the Holy One of God, the Saint of saints, consecrated by the Holy Spirit, who dwelt within Him. Mary and St. Joseph knew that the Son of God desired from the first to act like other men; that He wished from His birth to show them an example of true virtue, and that He would not exempt Himself from any law. He Himself dictated that law to His servant Moses on Mount Sinai, and yet He submitted to it humbly like the least of His children. This then was the distinguished name by which the Lord was to be known in this world: *Jesus*, which means " He shall save His people from their sins." He saved them by washing away their sins, by imparting to them the grace of suc-

cessfully resisting temptation, by conducting His
followers to a place of heavenly bliss where sin is
excluded. To know, then, whether we belong to
those to whom Jesus is a Saviour, we must examine whether we desire to be saved from sin,
whether we regard sin as the greatest evil on earth,
and whether, consequently, we are determined to
renounce it with all the energy of our souls.

Such is the meaning of the adorable name of
Jesus, a name which God has raised above all
names ; a name at which " every knee should bow
of those that are in heaven, on earth, and under
the earth " (Phil. ii. 10). St. Paul asserts that
this sacred name cannot be pronounced worthily
but by the grace of the Holy Ghost.

St. Bernard says of the holy name : " Blessed
name ! Oil flowing softly over the whole earth !
From heaven it flowed to Judea, from Judea over
the whole world. How striking the likeness of
oil to the name of Jesus ! Oil has three qualities :
it illuminates when burned, it nourishes when
consumed, it heals when applied to wounds. So,
too, the name of Jesus : it illuminates when He
preaches, nourishes when He protects, heals when
He is invoked. How could you explain this sud-
den spread of the light of faith over the world but
through the name of Jesus ? What more effec-

tually nourishes our courage, what strengthens our virtue and maintains morality, what promotes chaste self-control, what fills the soul with sweetness and vigor as the name of Jesus ? Is one of us sad or timid, in danger, or perhaps in sin ? behold ! as soon as the name of Jesus enters his heart and ascends to his lips all gloom vanishes before the light and the anxious sinner breathes a new life. Insipid is that food which is not seasoned with the oil of the name of Jesus. I take no pleasure in anything that may be written except I read there the name of Jesus. No words you may address to me will excite my interest unless I hear among them the name of Jesus. Jesus is honey in my mouth, music in my ear, and joy to my heart. Always carry this name in thy breast, as He Himself directs : ' Put Me as a seal upon thy heart, as a seal upon thy arm ' " (Cant. viii. 6).

Sweet, amiable Infant Jesus ! With Thy Mother and St. Joseph, I adore Thee, lying in a manger ; with the shepherds, I kneel at Thy feet and acknowledge Thee, the Saviour of the world ; with the Magi, I come from afar, guided by faith to Thy humble cave, and offer there my gifts of gold, my best actions, my life in fact. I offer there the incense of adoration ; to my God I offer the myrrh of penance and mortification.

The Presentation of the Child Jesus in the Temple. The Purification of the Blessed Virgin.

AFTER the birth of a son, according to the law of Moses, there was prescribed for the Jewish mother a term of purification. This time she passed in seclusion, and when the period was over she had to make her first journey with her child to the Temple ; the mother to be purified, and the first-born son to be offered to God. The mother was obliged to make an offering of a lamb a year old, or, if she were poor, a dove. When the fulness of time had arrived, Joseph and Mary went to Jerusalem, she to be purified according to the law, and the Child to be consecrated unreservedly to the service of God.

Now at this time there was in Jerusalem a just man, one who feared God, named Simeon, who lived in expectation of the consolation of Israel. It had been revealed to him by the Holy Ghost that he should not die before he had seen Christ the Lord. Simeon was a wise and learned scribe,

well versed in the Scriptures, as the scribes had to
be, for they interpreted authoritatively the law of
God. As Mary and Joseph were approaching, the
Spirit moved Simeon also to go to the Temple,
and they met at the gate. Nothing in the exterior
of Jesus, Mary, and Joseph distinguished them
from the rest of mankind; but the Holy Ghost
spoke to the old man, and when he met them face
to face, he saw at once in the Child the coming
Messias. His eyes were opened, and with a soul
full of consolation he burst forth in this canticle
of the divine Spirit:

"Now Thou dost deliver Thy servant, O Lord,
according to Thy word in peace : Because my eyes
have seen Thy salvation, that salvation which
Thou hast prepared before the face of all peoples.
A light to the revelation of the Gentiles, and the
glory of Thy people Israel."

This great hymn, which is known better perhaps by the first Latin words "Nunc dimittis," is
so simple, so holy, there is such a desire in it to
be dissolved and to be with God, that it is used in
the burial services. It is one of the psalms of the
canonical evening prayers. It revealed the fact
that Simeon wished to die, but could not until he
should see Christ as God had made known to him.
St. Joseph and the Blessed Virgin were aston-

ished that he was so clearly inspired with the dignity of the Child. Simeon held the Child in his arms. " Behold," said he, " this Child is set for the fall and for the resurrection of many in Israel," that is, He shall live to be contradicted by the Jews, who, by their sinful obstinacy, will bring eternal damnation on themselves. Then turning to Mary, he said : " Thy own soul a sword shall pierce that out of many hearts thoughts may be revealed." The Gospel says of him : " This man was just and devout, waiting for the consolation of Israel, and the Holy Ghost was in him."

When these things were going on in the Temple, one quiet old woman was witness of it all. " There was one Anna a prophetess, the daughter of Phanuel, of the tribe of Aser : she was far advanced in years, and had lived with her husband seven years from her virginity. And she was a widow until fourscore and four years : who departed not from the Temple, by fastings and prayers serving night and day. Now she at the same hour coming in, confessed to the Lord : and spoke of Him to all that looked for the redemption of Israel " (Luke ii. 36–38).

To Mary and Joseph, these events were consoling because it made them understand that God was in a hidden and humble way working secretly in behalf of His divine Son. "And after they had performed all things according to the law of the Lord, they returned into Galilee, to their city Nazareth."

In the presentation of Jesus and the purification of the Mother of God, we admire their obedience and their great humility. Though Jesus was not bound by any precept of the Old Law, still Mary did not excuse herself from "fulfilling everything according to the law of the Lord."

The feast of the Purification of the Blessed Virgin is celebrated on the second of February, and is known as Candlemas-day. On that day candles are blessed by the priests, and the faithful take them home to burn when any sacrament is given; for according to the law of the Church a wax candle must be burning while the priest is administering a sacrament. Candles are also used at a death, to show us that the soul lives though the body may be dead, that faith carries the light from this world to the other life. Again, pious people use them in severe thunder-storms, showing their lively trust in God's mercy, when the elements appear to express the anger of God and threaten destruction.

O Jesus, Light of the world, enlighten my mind that I may follow in Thy light, and persevere all through my life to imitate Thy glorious examples of virtue, and that my life may be a light that will shine for the edification of all who see it.

Mary also, as the sorrowful Mother, is not to be forgotten. We often see the Blessed Virgin represented in pictures with a sword piercing her heart ; oftener we find the heart of Mary pierced with seven swords, as not only one sorrow entered the heart of Mary, but she had to endure many pangs. Under the title of sorrowful Mother, her children love to come to her, because they think that having suffered so much in conjunction with the Passion of Our Lord, her sorrows and her prayers will plead most eloquently before the throne of God in their behalf.

> At the cross her station keeping
> Stood the mournful Mother weeping,
>   Close to Jesus to the last.
> Through her heart, His sorrow sharing,
> All His bitter anguish bearing,
>   Lo! the piercing sword has passed!

The Massacre of the Holy Innocents.

HEROD waited for the Magi to return and tell him of their success in finding the new-born King of the Jews ; but he waited in vain. He saw now that he had been deceived, and at once determined to put into execution the resolution he had made at the coming of the Magi into Jerusalem, namely, that of putting to death all the male children of two years and under, so as to make sure that Christ was among them. This cruelty need not surprise us, as Herod was a very wicked tyrant. During his reign he had his wife and two sons put to death. This massacre of the children is an historical fact, because it is related in the Gospel, but the manner of its execution or the number of victims is not known. The most natural supposition is that soldiers were sent to Bethlehem and the neighborhood and butchered the children with their swords. St. Augustine, in a sermon on the massacre of the holy innocents, says : " When the Lord was born, sorrow began, not for heaven, but for the world. Mothers wept, but angels rejoiced. God is born; He who came to condemn the malice of the world needed innocent victims. Lambs are sacrificed, because the Lamb of God is to be crucified. The sheep bleat because they are deprived of their offspring."

Grand is the martyrdom, although the spectacle is a cruel one. Mothers sought by every means to hide their little ones, but they in their innocence gave evidence of their presence. They knew not the value of silence. The poor mothers cried out to the executioners, "Why do you separate me from him to whom I gave birth? Has he without purpose sought nourishment at my breast? With what care have I tended to that dear child whom you toss about with such cruelty! You have disembowelled him and dashed him to the earth." One cried out: "Why do you not kill me with the child? why do you leave me? If there is any crime, it is I who have committed it; if there is no crime, kill us both if it must be." Another said: "For whom are you seeking? You are looking for one Child, and you kill many; but Him you will not find." Others again cried: "Come, oh, come, Saviour of the world! how long dost Thou defer Thy coming? Thou fearest no one, do not allow our children to be murdered." The lamentations of the mothers ascended to heaven and the sacrifice of the little ones accompanied them.

Truly the prophecy quoted by St. Matthew was fulfilled : " A voice in Rama was heard, lamentation and great mourning ; Rachel bewailing her children and would not be comforted, because they are not." Consider the sorrow with which the divine Infant is penetrated at the death of these innocent victims, slaughtered for His sake ; it was revealed to St. Bridget that the Blessed Virgin was thrown into great anguish at hearing of this massacre.

The slaughter of the innocents made little stir in Judea, for the poor Jews often suffered from the wholesale cruelty practised on them ; but they were powerless to resent it, and the spirit of opposition and hate to their governors became the greater. Antiquity had little respect for babyhood, so that nowhere do we find mention made of this act of cruelty except in the Gospel. Legend tells us that, in order to make his work easier and more certain, Herod invited all the mothers of Bethlehem to a feast in his palace at Jerusalem ; they were to bring their children under two years old that they might receive a gift. The unsuspecting mothers came in throngs and in holiday attire. When all were within the building, and it was securely locked, Herod's executioners rushed in among the horror-stricken mothers, tore their children from their arms, and murdered them before their eyes. Their bodies were thrown into a large pit, and then the mothers were allowed to go their way. As these holy innocents died for Christ's sake, they are the first martyrs.

Hail! first flowers of martyrdom! Holy innocents! Little witnesses to the divinity of the Infant Jesus! Little roses dyed with glorious purple! Dear little ones of Bethlehem, patrons and protectors of Christian children, pray for us, that in our childhood we may give testimony of our faith, that we may also be innocent and love the Infant Jesus with a great love.

Almighty God punished Herod, even in this life, as he deserved, but a greater punishment of eternal damnation awaited him in the other world. A horrid disease began to consume his body; the corruption of the tomb devoured him during life. He sought relief from doctors and from healing baths; but all to no purpose. He made an attempt on his own life; when he regained consciousness and found he was near his end he gave orders that several of the best families of Jerusalem should be killed, so that tears might be shed at his funeral. But he died, and the last cruel order was not executed.

The Flight into Egypt.

To frustrate the malicious designs of Herod,
God sent an angel to Joseph in his sleep, who said:
"Arise, and take the Child and His Mother and
fly into Egypt. There you will dwell until such
time as I shall declare to you, for Herod is searching for the Child to destroy Him." Joseph in-
stantly rose from his bed, and, taking the Child
and His Mother, set forth on his journey.

Away from the land of God, the land of their
forefathers, they hastened in the darkness, fugi-
tives from the cruel pursuit of an enemy. How
and where they went no one knows; the indication
is that they went into Egypt: how far into
that land they penetrated is not known; we are
certain that they must have gone into this country, for there they were protected from the power
of Herod, under the laws of a foreign country.
Their journey had to be made in haste, for Bethlehem was but two hours' distant from Jerusalem,
and at any moment the soldiers might arrive and
cut off their retreat: no doubt the massacre was

ordered immediately after the departure of the Magi had become known, and moreover, even then there might have been spies about to locate the whereabouts of the divine Child. The jealousy which devoured the mind of Herod prompted him to secure his throne by whatever cruel means came first to his hand. The Gospel tells us nothing of this flight, for nothing very strange happened to make any particular circumstance worthy of record. The long stretches of the desert witnessed the passage of the Holy Family ; at first they avoided coming in contact with the people and took refuge in old buildings or perhaps even under the canopy of heaven. The painters and poets of the past have drawn fanciful pictures of dangers into which they ran, the robbers whom they met, the lions and tigers which came near them, but instead of showing their natural ferocity, only showed that they instinctively knew the Master of the universe. The palm trees not only gave them shelter, but bowed down their heads to make it easy to get at the fruit.

In Cairo is shown an old church which from time immemorial is designated as the temporary habitation of the Holy Family in Egypt. Here is shown an ancient dwelling of two rooms and an alcove, used by them, the place where Mary and the Infant Jesus retired and where Joseph had his separate lodging. There in the garden is also shown a tree of very great age, which to this day is called the Virgin's tree. However, it is not known why St. Joseph should have selected this spot for the sojourn of the Holy Family when the borders of the foreign land would have rendered all the necessary security.

Then word came to St. Joseph that he should return to his home. Gladly indeed did these exiles return to Palestine. On their way they did not know where to direct their steps. Archelaus, Herod's son, was now governor of Judea, and keeping at a distance from the city of Bethlehem, the dreaded place, the Holy Family made Nazareth happy by their presence. It was their old home, Joseph's parents and relatives had lived there, perhaps he even had property of his own there, for they inhabited the house that afterwards became famous, which is called the Holy House of Nazareth, and is now at Loretto.

The Life of Our Lord in Nazareth. The Holy Family.

TRADITION has it that Joseph was a carpenter by trade. St. Hilary thinks he worked in iron, making yokes and ploughs, but in the East at that time most of the agricultural implements were made of wood, and Joseph was able to work the little iron used about them. In many villages of Palestine where laborers are scarce, it is a general practice to combine several trades; and thus St. Joseph worked sometimes in his shop, and at other times went out to do the little woodwork a house required. Those Eastern houses were mostly of stone; the roof was of stone, and stone steps from the outside led to the top of the house. Mary stayed at home, an admirable mother of the family, fit model for all who have charge of a house; working, too, as tradition tells us, to contribute her share to the scanty support that Joseph could scrape together: her spare hours occupied in spinning linen and weaving it into cloth. The first Christians are said to have preserved

141

beautiful specimens of her handiwork. Did not
Our Lord, in His sermons, perhaps refer to this
diligent housewife who made the dough and hid
the leaven in it and watched it until it was all
leavened and risen to its proper height ? He referred to the economical manager who mends the
worn garment, who sweeps the house with care ;
the neat housekeeper who cleanses the vessels; the
charitable widow who gives from the little she has.
She is the strong woman of the Old Testament,
as contemplative as Magdalen. She it was who,
according to the custom of those days, ground the
wheat for bread and prepared the frugal meal of
fresh fish, dried meats, fruits, herbs boiled in
water, milk and honey. At certain times of the
day she, more beautiful than Rebecca, went to
the fountain, which is shown to this day and ven-
erated by pilgrims, to draw water for household
use.

Jesus was there in His infant grace and loveliness to contribute to the social life of Joseph
and Mary. His loving arms often encircled His
Mother's neck in a tender embrace ; His tongue
was loosed, and He began to talk in adorable
words to those who were near and dear to Him.
In His innocent play He follows father and
mother and sees them working at their duties; He

asks them questions and astonishes them by His
heavenly wisdom. You can imagine the divine
Child playing in the workshop of Joseph among
the shavings, and forming of little wooden blocks
a model of the cross on which He was to die; even
His shadow making startling portents of the future. You can see Him lightly tripping to the
fountain with Mary or to the woods with Joseph,
carrying the smaller tools or other necessaries for
his trade.

What beautiful scenes these are, which we naturally suppose that angelic visitors often looked
upon with rapture ; how lovely were those meals
taken in common; how holy the prayers that were
said together! When the day was over these three
holy ones sat down to table with affection and joy.
Their conversation sometimes grave, sometimes
joyful, but always sweet, found subject enough in
the incidents of the day ; reminiscences of the
flight into Egypt and other pious subjects passed
the time pleasantly. Joseph loved to speak of that
great providence of God, of which he had so many
proofs. Mary spoke of the coming events of the
life of Our Lord, and He must have opened her
mind that she might see distinctly the course of the
events. It was perhaps from such beautiful enter-
tainments at their meals that Our Lord so easily

passed into the scenes of His after life; working His first miracle at the marriage feast of Cana, receiving the sinner Magdalen and forgiving her sins at the table of the Pharisee, instituting the Blessed Eucharist at the last supper.

After the evening repast came the hour of prayer; the quiet hours were spent on the roofs of the houses, fitted for the purpose. Peace reigned amid the Holy Family, the stars shone out brightly, and silence came over the streets. Joseph and Mary did not have to seek God in the immensity of the universe; He was there in human form, His face radiant with the love of His Father; awake or asleep the glory of God shone on Him. They did not speak to Him of His divinity; they poured out no praises on His sacred person; He was still a child and, according to the will of God, He had to grow out of His childhood before He would reveal Himself. But Mary and Joseph felt an indescribable emotion when they looked upon that divine Youth. The three holy ones remained together in silent ecstasy in which they saw the heavens opened and the glory of the Son of man shining brighter than the sun. Then all prostrated themselves in adoration of God, the divine Child mingling His prayers with theirs. In the vast silence of the night Heaven bent down to listen to their humble supplications; they seemed to be the echoes of the adoration of the choirs of angels. The powerful cry now began to arise to heaven, that cry which in after days was to continue, and find mercy for the human race.

Jesus among the Doctors.

WHEN Jesus was about twelve years old, a very interesting incident took place; it is related at some length by St. Luke, and means something. Perhaps it is to show that all through the life of Christ incidents like this took place, which are not recorded because they had no relation to the establishment of the religion of Jesus. Another idea in it may be to show that, when the Child came to the use of reason, He was taught to subject Himself to the law of Moses, and was instructed by the rabbis in the manner of observing the Jewish laws, customs, and ceremonies. Hence it is that Jesus, who was now twelve years old, accompanied Joseph and Mary to the Temple in Jerusalem, according to the law. Of course only the Jews within a reasonable limit were obliged to come to Jerusalem. On the Feast of Pentecost, and the Feast of the Tabernacles too, the pious Jew would take his whole family and wander slowly towards the sacred city. On this occasion it was the Pasch on which Our Lord visited Jerusalem. "His

parents went every year to Jerusalem, at the solemn day of the Pasch. And when He was twelve
years old, they going up into Jerusalem according
to the custom of the feast, and having fulfilled the
days, when they returned the Child Jesus remained in Jerusalem, and His parents knew it not.
And thinking that He was in the company, they
came a day's journey, and sought Him among
their kinsfolk and acquaintance. And not finding
Him, they returned into Jerusalem, seeking Him.
And it came to pass, that after three days they
found Him in the Temple sitting in the midst of
the doctors, hearing them and asking them questions. And all that heard Him were astonished
at His wisdom and His answers " (Luke ii. 41-47).
Mary and Joseph, in great consternation, retraced
their steps to Jerusalem, and reached the city just
at daybreak. In pain and sorrow they hurried
through the streets, searching and inquiring
everywhere for the Child, but all in vain. Thus
for three weary days they wandered up and down
on their sad errand. They were full of grief, while
He, their Child, was seemingly enjoying peace and
happiness in the Temple of Jerusalem when they
found Him. No wonder then that Mary broke
out into just complaint at what she considered her
Son's thoughtlessness. And seeing Him they

wondered, and His Mother said to Him, " Son,
why hast Thou done so to us ? Behold Thy father
and I have sought Thee sorrowing."   Joseph and
Mary wondered that Jesus, a mere boy, was there
among the doctors, but still commanding so much
respect that these wise and learned doctors humbly answered every question which He gave them.
Not only did He ask questions, but He pro-
pounded the sacred texts so clearly to the doctors
of the law that they marvelled at the erudition
of this Child, this carpenter's son.

Great was the relief and joy of Mary and Joseph
when they beheld their beloved Son ; and Our
Lord, turning to Mary, calmly said : " How is
it that you sought Me ? Did you not know that
I must be about My Father's business? " Mary and
Joseph knew that Jesus was the Son of God, and
was on this earth for the redemption of mankind
—to reconcile humanity to the Father. Now, indeed, He had come to the use of reason according
to the flesh, and now was the time to declare em-
phatically that all His acts hereafter were to be
sacrifices to God. His whole life after this in its
every smallest detail was in accordance with these
words, " Did you not know I must be about My
Father's business ? "   There is no obstinacy in
these words of Jesus ; they give the reason for His

conduct in remaining in Jerusalem unknown to
them. The God-man must from henceforth be occupied with God's honor and glory. God's interests
are to be His life's occupation. His time for public
appearance had not yet come ; the time of subjection, of obedience and of retirement, was to
continue without interruption to the day of His
final separation, when He should reach the age at
which a man may begin to teach. " And He went
down with them and came to Nazareth, and was
subject to them." There was no exception to His
obedience ; it extended to everything.

'Twas the week of the Passover: only
  The aged, the sickly, the blind,
The tottering children, and lonely
  Young mothers, had tarried behind.
To sacredest feast of the nation,
  Through the paths that their fathers had trod,
All others, with paschal oblation,
  Had gone to the city of God.

The seven days' festival ended,
  Rites finished for people and priest,
The throngs from the Temple descended,
  And homeward set face from the feast.
And neighbor had converse with neighbor,
  Unwonted and simple and free,
As northward they journeyed towards Thabor,
  Or westward they turned to the sea.

But not till the night-dews were falling
  Did Mary, oft-questioning, find,
As children to children were calling,
  That Jesus had lingered behind.
He vex her—the Mother that bore Him?
  Or veiled it some portent or sign?
For oft had she trembled before Him,
  Her human too near His divine.

She sought midst her kinsfolk, whose pity
  Grew tender to look on her grief;
Then back through the streets of the city
  She hastened, yet found not relief.
Thus searching, a marvellous story
  Her ear and her senses beguiled:
"The rabbis, gray-bearded and hoary,
  In the Temple are taught by a Child!"

O marvel of womanly weakness!
  She finds Him,—fears, sorrows, subside,
And Mary, the angel of meekness,
  In petulance pauses to chide:
"Son, wherefore thus tarry to gather
  About Thee the curious throng,
Unheeding, the while, that Thy father
  And I have been seeking Thee long?"

A look so reproachingly tender,
  It awed while it melted her eye,
He cast, as He hastened to render
  Subjection and filial reply:
"Nay, wherefore perplexed and pursuing?
  Dost thou too, My Mother, forget
And wist not the Son must be doing
  The work that His Father hath set?"

—M. J. Preston.

Mary and Joseph did not understand the words of Our Lord ; it had not been revealed to them how the redemption of man was to be effected, but they engraved His words on their hearts. They knew He belonged to them by obedience for a while longer, but that the day would come when all would be made clear to them ; Mary believed, trusted, loved, and adored with all the powers of her soul. "And He went down with them, and came to Nazareth, and was subject to them ; and Jesus advanced in wisdom and age and grace with God and man."

The Boyhood of Jesus.

Head so light upon my breast,
  Heart so quick against my own!
Can it be that God doth rest
  Here, so babe-like, narrow-grown?

Flaky, glowing hair has He,
  Breath like faintest jasmine sighs.
Dreams, enchant my Dear for me;
  Sleep, soon veil my Baby's eyes!

NAZARETH was the quiet home of the Son of
God for many years. He was like other boys
exteriorly. The boyhood as well as the incarnation is a mystery, as is the whole life of
Christ. We believe with a firm faith that Jesus
is the Son of God, that He is as great a God as
God the Father or the Holy Ghost ; that He is
infinitely wise and infinitely mighty; on the other
hand, we read in the Gospel that Jesus was a real
child, that He grew in age, in grace, and in wisdom. None of these truths involve a contradic-
tion; they are indeed beyond our reason, but faith
comes to our assistance. The interior life of Christ

as a boy was full of the thoughts of God ; the exterior was the same as other children's. Bossuet, the great preacher, says : " Thou lovely Babe ! Happy were they who gazed upon Thee, stretching forth Thy arms from out the swaddling-bands, lifting up Thy little fingers to caress Thy holy Mother. Now upheld by her strong arms adventuring Thy first short steps, now practising Thy holy tongue with stammerings of the praise of God, Thy Father !

" I worship Thee, dear Child, at every stage of Thy divine growth ; the while Thou art nursed at her pure breast or with wails of infancy dost call for her, or repose on her bosom clasped in her warm arms."

Nazareth is in Galilee, a beautiful village on the side of a hill; it is said that Palestine has no more smiling landscape than this little valley of Nazareth. Antonius, the martyr, compared it to paradise.

" Can anything of good come from Nazareth ? " asked Nathanael of Philip when Our Lord called them to the apostleship. Nazareth was an insignificant place : the last in the world from which to expect anything very great. It is certainly remarkable that this place, the dearest to the Christian heart of all places on earth, except perhaps Jerusalem, is not mentioned in the Old Testament. It was probably a very small hamlet, hidden away in the narrow valley and of no political importance. It must, however, ever be a spot sacred to the whole Christian world, for here our blessed Saviour passed the greater part of His life on earth. Here the Child Jesus grew from infancy to childhood and youth, and in knowledge and favor with God and man. Here He spent the years of His ripening manhood in humble labors and in sinless communion with God. What natural desires arise in our mind to lift the veil that shrouds this period in impenetrable darkness! The narrow vale, on the side of which the village is built, is the same as it was in the time of Our Lord. The view from the village is circumscribed, but from the summit of the hills could be seen the distant sea and many places mentioned in the Scriptures.

All that is known of the child-life of Jesus in this place is comprised in the words of St. Luke: "The Child grew, and waxed strong, full of wisdom; and the grace of God was in Him." This is the period of the life of Christ in which, while He grew like other children, His soul also progressed.

How are we to understand this interior development of Jesus? The common feeling is that His wisdom and His power declared themselves by degrees, although He possessed them in their plenitude from His conception. Still we must remember that Our Saviour not only wished to appear as a child, but to be a child according to nature. It is the law of childhood that as the body develops little by little, so the intelligence grows with the strength of the body. It is a sacred mystery to which we bow with perfect submission of our understanding. Jesus is truly God, the Infinite, the All-Knowing and Omnipresent, and yet, circumscribed by the narrow limits of a weak human form, He is really a child ; He grows in age, in grace, and in wisdom.

Outwardly there was nothing at this time of His life to distinguish Jesus from other children : and the child-life of Christ passed serenely in the quiet abode of Nazareth. Here He received from Mary and Joseph the simple lessons which the law prescribed ; He learned to read the Scriptures, heard them explained, and apparently learned them, because He was growing in age and wisdom. The Scriptures speak of Him, they lead and point to Him ; Mary and Joseph knew it well, but they never failed in their duty of teaching Him and meditating with Him on the word of God contained in the Old Testament.

Perhaps as Jesus enlightened the doctors of the law on the prophecies, so also He made His earthly guardians aware of the hidden application of them to Himself. What great thoughts and ideas did this intimate relationship of mind give them ! how Mary and Joseph treasured the knowledge in their hearts. During these years of sojourn together in greatest intimacy they felt a happiness, a consolation, and a peace that was beyond anything they could imagine in store for them through the mercy of God. The beatific vision was ever before Jesus, He was ever in close union with the eternal Father, and Mary especially participated in these flights of the soul from this vale of tears. If the saints were privileged to a higher union with God, how much closer to God were these privileged beings, so intimate with the Child Jesus on this earth ! He was an open-hearted, good, noble boy. We can hardly imagine a more agreeable person than such a child. How often must He have found it almost impossible to sink His omnipotence, and let the human side predominate when He beheld the misery about Him; when He saw the poverty of so many; when He saw sickness and death visiting fond parents or even His own companions and playfellows ! With the patience and long-suffering of a God He permitted these things even though He could have averted them ; but, as now, His holy providence watching over every one, allowed all to happen for their own good. As in His after-life we see Jesus working a miracle and forbidding the people to speak of it, that it might be kept secret, so in His boyhood He worked miracles of holy providence in secret. Wherever He went He brought blessings and happiness. Like the ark that accidentally brought a blessing to the house of Obededom, so Jesus was doing good now, though the fame of it did not go abroad. " He hath done all things well " (Mark vii. 37).

"Jesus Waxed and Grew Strong."

THE Child Jesus grew in stature, in character, in learning, in experience, even in goodness. He did not stand still; it was remarkable what progress He made. Although it is God Himself who is revealed to us in the life of Jesus Christ, yet this did not prevent Him from being made like unto us in all things, sin only excepted.

> Was not Our Lord a little child,
> Taught by degrees to pray;
> By father dear and Mother mild,
> Instructed day by day?

Jesus grew to be a larger and a stronger boy every day; He made Himself useful as soon as the playfulness of childhood had passed. He was frequently found in the workshop of St. Joseph, helping at the work of the day. But you, dear children, are daily growing also; you are getting away from childhood, and a more serious life is before you: you can now make

yourselves useful ; you must now learn to help
your parents in many things. We often see boys
in stores, running on errands, carrying bundles,
and earning a livelihood ; not getting much for
their work, but getting a little for their faithfulness and taking it home, like little men, glad that
they can contribute their share to the support
of the family. By degrees such boys will be advanced in the business ; they will learn the various branches of it, and finally, after years, may
become members of a great firm. This is a physical and business growth which is very useful in its
own way.

There is another growth, that of the soul, of a
moral character, where you are no longer a child,
when you have outgrown the playfulness and
thoughtlessness of the infant ; you have a growth
before you and a very important one. You have
to become a man, you have to grow to a certain
excellence, so that you may command the respect
of all you come in contact with. We know that
a man of sense, of religion, of education, of spirit,
is respected and has considerable weight with his
fellow beings : well, that is the very thing you
must aim at and strive to gain, that you may be
a worthy member of society. And this growth is
beginning now in your youth and will continue.

who knows how long? at least until you have grown into manhood. You are neither an infant nor have you arrived at mature sense. The present is an intermediate time which is to be given over to growth. Everything is arranged by your parents, by the Church, by the school, and by every one interested in your welfare, that this growth may be healthy and continuous. You notice that your parents want you to learn; that in school, books are put into your hands; and that you must learn your prayers and your catechism. You are growing now, for all this learning, this training, is a growth, and a very important growth, because you have to attain such a high excellence. You are beginning now to realize your existence, you are becoming self-conscious, you feel that you are here for a purpose, and that you have certain duties to perform; you begin to feel that you are obliged to attend to these duties. You are responsible for your acts to God and to man, and you may make man interested in you or God a friend, according to your conduct. You have the law of God to consider; you have, moreover, to consider the desires of your parents, and you must respect the laws of the land, even though you may not know them yet. You can, in short, be a saint, a good man, or a bad, useless wreck of a man. You

are no longer an infant, and at the same time you
are far from the wisdom of age. Consequently,
though your parents no longer carry you in their
arms, you have not yet the wisdom of age, and
need to be shown what you must do. Your parents
let you walk by yourself, but they tell you which
way to take. How beautiful is your life if you
begin it right! What more beautiful thing is
there in this world than a good-hearted, generous
boy, intelligent and willing? What is there more
lovely than a happy, smiling, bright girl showing
respectful affection to all about her? If there is
anything that makes this world attractive in certain aspects it is to see and come in contact with
good children. These little people are yet innocent of the wiles of the world; they are guileless,
satisfied, and have little to complain of; one can
enjoy their company, which is not always the case
with older people. You are loved at this age by
every one. God, especially, loves you. When God
the Father created you He gave you at the same
time a guardian angel. So precious are you in His
sight that to make sure that you do not go astray
He deputes an angel to look after you. The doc-
trine of the guardian angel was told you long ago.
Among the first prayers you said was that to your
guardian angel.

Blest spirits of light, O, ye have not forsaken
  The children of earth and the fallen from bliss.
Thou still watchest round us, our bosoms awaken
  To thoughts of a world that is brighter than this.
O, fondly watch o'er us! O, guard and protect us!
  Blest angels, direct us to mansions of bliss.

Who loves you more than Jesus Our Saviour?
The Child Jesus sanctified your station and period
of life by living it Himself. As yet, however,
it is a very imperfect life, because it is not
fully developed; that only is perfect which is
fully developed. But Our Lord always remembered His childhood, and even when He was a
serious man engaged in the work for which He
came to this world, when He was preaching the
new gospel, He still remembered it. There was
quite a scene once among the apostles. They were
disputing who was to be the greatest among them;
there was jealousy and disagreement, and, perhaps,
hot words about precedence. They all wanted to
be the first. It was a dispute which must have
grieved Our Lord very much. But He took a
child, and placing him in the midst of them, said,
"Unless you become as little children, you shall
not enter the kingdom of heaven." So we see that
even grown people must remain as little children
if they wish to go to heaven. At another time

Our Lord was caressing little children and playing
with them, and mothers were bringing still other
children, and sending them toddling along until
they reached the good Master. The apostles were
angry about it, and wished to prevent it, for, perhaps, they thought Our Lord might be better employed than in fondling children. Our good Lord
turned to them and said, " Suffer the children to
come to Me and forbid them not, for of such is
the kingdom of God." Just because Our Lord
sanctified childhood, therefore has He merited for
you the grace to grow as He did in all those beautiful virtues of which He gives us an example in
His youth.

In your youth, too, are you much loved by the
Third Person of Godhead, the Holy Ghost. You
are made His holy abode. No sooner were you
born than you were taken to the church: you were
a being that belonged first to the Church more
than anywhere else. In the Church you were
consecrated to God by the Sacrament of Baptism.
You were made an heir of the kingdom of God,
you were made a child of God. Because you
were a child, you had a right to all that God has.
You were baptized to show that Jesus Christ the
Son of God is your brother ; you belong to the
same family of children of God with Him, and

when you became a Christian, a Catholic, you promised to remain faithful to this choice.

Lastly you were baptized in the name of the Holy Ghost, the Third Person of the Blessed Trinity. You were to be the habitation of God ; the Father, and the Son, and the Holy Ghost are to come to your heart to stay there, and you are to love them and allow yourself to be led by their inspiration. You must allow nothing but God to be the Master of your soul : because the Holy Ghost only is to be there by right of possession.

We understand now how Jesus grew : He was born an infant and His days were spent in God's service until His body had grown to its years, fit for a sacrifice to God on the cross. You know now also, my dear children, that Jesus grew in wisdom and grace before God and man; that day after day as this divine Youth grew older He manifested to men a wisdom which was fitted to His age and at the same time astonished them by its perfection. Now is the time in your tender years, when you bestow your affections so easily, to give the Lord your hearts and love Him also who has loved you so much. Let the Infant Jesus make your hearts flourish with beautiful virtues and with the fruits of good actions. Avoid doing wrong, do not practise the vices of bad children :

for these vices make them abominable before God and man. We all dislike bad children and are disgusted that they have learned vice so very early in life.

The Piety of Joseph and Mary.

WE may well imagine that the days of sojourn in Nazareth were days of peace and happiness, until the Son of man having begun His sacred mission at last ascended the heights of Calvary to die on the cross. This, according to the Fathers of the Church, is the epitome of the infancy of Jesus: when two years old He was weaned; at three years He walked ; at four, He made the home happy by His presence ; at six, He began to speak admirable words of wisdom, and at seven and eight, He rejoiced all by His innocent conduct. It appears probable that Our Lord did not dwell alone in that quiet home of Nazareth ; He had relatives living there or in the neighborhood. How closely they were related is not certain ; perhaps they were cousins, or it may be their relationship was still more distant. We know, however, that in those days relations were called brothers ; but whether this relationship was near or distant has never been well defined. We read in St. Mark (vi. 3) that the townspeople pretended to know all about Our

Lord, for they said, " Are not His brethren James, Joseph, Simon, and Jude ? And are not His sisters all here among us ? "

Among these Our Lord lived ; some of them became apostles, as James and Jude ; the former was called the Just and the latter Thaddeus, "Man of the heart." These were the most distinguished, because they took an active part in the extension of the Gospel. But the other relatives, as St. John sorrowfully says, did not believe in Him ; they even mocked Him, saying, " Pass from hence, and go into Judea : that Thy disciples also may see Thy works which Thou dost. For there is no man that doth anything in secret, and he himself seeketh to be known openly ; if Thou do these things, manifest Thyself to the world." These men and women had no higher ambition than to enjoy the world. When Our Lord began to preach, they said, " He is gone mad." No doubt in course of time they followed Christ and believed in Him ; but at the period of the youth of Our Lord, their thoughts were not on His divine mission, they were more engrossed by the things of this earth than the things of heaven.

Praise, praise to Jesus, Mary, Joseph,
The three on earth most like to Thee in heaven!

Praise, praise to Jesus, Mary, Joseph,
  To whom these heavenly likenesses were given!
  Come, Christians, come, sweet anthems weaving;
  Come, young and old, come, gay or grieving;
      Praise, praise with me,
      Adoring and believing,
  God's Family, God's Holy Family!
                                    —*Rev. F. W. Faber.*

The Holy House of Loretto.

THE house in which the Holy Family spent so many years in Nazareth is indeed a sacred relic; it still exists and is highly prized. There is a singular history connected with it, and the facts are well authenticated. The Holy House is no longer in Nazareth, for in the year 1291 it was transported entire, by the ministry of angels, to Tersatz on the eastern coast of the Adriatic. At that time the house had disappeared from its foundations and was found in this town : declarations are made that angels were seen high up in the air carrying a house. In 1295 the angels again took up the house and carried it across the waters to Loretto, where it now is. The angels themselves seem to consider this house a very precious relic, and they are so interested in it that they have located it on the spot where it is now. The Holy House is not a very large building : it is twenty-seven feet long and twelve feet wide; it is of broad, thin red brick. It stands now in the centre of a beautiful church of the walled town of Loretto :

as we enter the church there stands before us a marble house with rich and artistic carvings around it, portraying the life of the Holy Family in the various scenes for which we have scriptural authority ; this marble house screens the real one entirely, so that you cannot see it or touch it.

But why did not the angels keep this Holy House in Nazareth, where it really belongs ? We can hardly answer this, except that it showed the interest God Himself felt in this Holy House, and that it might not be desecrated by unholy hands, He had it removed to its present place. It certainly required supernatural power to bring it entire all that way from Nazareth, so many hundred miles, to its present position. For in those days the sacrilegious Turk was ruling over that country : he was destroying sanctuaries and turning them into mosques, he was persecuting the Christians, of whom many suffered martyrdom. In order, then, to bring it and keep it forever in a Catholic country God permitted this miracle to be wrought. What truth there is in the translation of the Holy House to Loretto we will not attempt to state, or on what grounds it is believed. This we know, that many Pontiffs have believed in the miraculous translation, have granted many indulgences to those who make pilgrimages to it, so

that very many who love the Blessed Virgin think
themselves happy to go there and pray in that
house as it is preserved to-day; they can gain plen-
ary indulgences there, and many miracles have
been and are continually wrought there. The
Litany of the Blessed Virgin, which we recite so
often, had its origin in Loretto.

The pious pilgrim enters this house with awe
and reverence and prays fervently, having before
his eyes the image of the Holy Family who once
dwelt there. It is asserted that the house rests
on no foundation, but miraculously hangs in the
air an inch from the ground, so that you can
pass an iron ruler under it, if you wish to convince
yourself that it is not connected with the earth.
Here also is shown a little earthenware bowl, from
which Our Lord is said to have taken His food
and which came with the Holy House. No wonder that this little house is held in such great
veneration, this home where the Child Jesus grew
up and prepared Himself for His great work !

The Death of St. Joseph.

It is not known when St. Joseph departed this life; probably in the designs of God this event took place when Our Lord was able to support Himself and His sweet Mother. The history of Joseph's death belongs to a time when Jesus was no longer a child; but it finds a very proper place here, because it happened before Our Lord's public life. According to tradition, St. Joseph reached a very old age; he was well on in years when he espoused the Blessed Virgin, and when his end came he felt no infirmity; his sight failed not, no tooth in his mouth decayed. The archangel Michael made known to him that his end was approaching. To prepare himself for the journey out of this world, he visited once more the holy Temple in Jerusalem, and prayed that the angel Michael would not desert him in his last moments, and that his guardian angel would stand by his side. When he returned to Nazareth he became very ill. Mary begged Our Lord to save St. Joseph's life, but He answered, " O, My most loving

Mother, on all men rests the sentence of death; thou also must expect the same end; but thy death and that of this good and just man is but the opening to eternal life; let us go, dearest Mother, and stand by his bedside that thou mayest see what happens when his soul goes out from the body." Both Mary and Jesus kept watch at St. Joseph's side. Our Lord comforted him in his dying moments, pointing to heaven where the angels were waiting to conduct him to the throne of God. Thus with the blessing of Our Lord and the supplications of Mary, the soul of Joseph left this world. What a happy death!

What are we to learn from the life of St. Joseph? Evidently great lessons are taught by his life of perseverance, humility, obedience, and prudence; great virtues, which you, my dear children, should learn early.

We see that steadfast perseverance with which St. Joseph endured all the privations and trials of his life. We, too, should learn to remain in the places and positions in which God has placed us, with the firm conviction that God's providence is watching over us. Often our imagination and our self-love make us resist the will of God; we would rather follow our own will. St. Joseph was without doubt one of the most perfect men that the world ever saw, and still almighty God sent him many trials; but he bore them nobly, because he saw the will of God in all. "Gold and silver are tried in the fire; and the favorites of God are tried in the oven of humility." Children should learn from St. Joseph unflinching obedience; it is the principal duty of children to do the will of their superiors, their parents, teachers, and pastors. A child becomes doubly beautiful and amiable by the readiness with which he practises obedience. You, my dear children, do not obey because you like to, but because it is the command of God. Our superiors hold the place of God: what they command on earth God ratifies in heaven, and it becomes His will.

Your rising in the morning, your going to bed at night, your school tasks, your prayers, are all commanded by your superiors. How often do you murmur in executing these precepts? St. Joseph never asked the reason why; willingly and quickly he did all that he was told to do, he performed all his duties in a most exact manner.

Let us pray with great fervor to this foster-father of Jesus, and take him for our model and patron. St. Teresa said that she never asked God for anything through St. Joseph without obtaining the favor.

Sing we Joseph, spouse of Mary,
  And our Mother's blessed friend;
Favors countless, mercies constant,
  Thou dost ever to us send.
We have prayed, and thou hast answered;
  We have asked, and thou hast given.
Need we marvel? Jesus tells us,
  Joseph has the stores of heaven.
One more favor we will ask thee,
  Thou of all canst grant it best:
When we die be thou still near us,
  Bring us safe to endless rest.

The Great Graces of St. Joseph's Soul.

ALL natural gifts are not to be compared in value to one supernatural grace. Great must have been the wealth of St. Joseph's soul. Graces without number were showered upon him for his fidelity to the work to which he was called.

The first great grace granted to this great saint was a virginal purity, by which he was made worthy to be the spouse of Mary and the father of Our Lord. Purity must surround that which is holy; nothing impure may approach before God. So that St. Joseph became a privileged guardian angel of the virginity of Our Lady. Instead of being an enemy of her eminent holiness he contributed to it: her virginal purity shines out much more decidedly. Not only was he the guardian of Mary, but also of Our Lord. St. Joseph was admitted to the pure embrace of the Child Jesus. "Blessed is the faithful and wise servant, for the Lord will place him over all His goods." When Our Saviour traversed the land of Judea, preaching, it was necessary only to touch the hem of His garment to be cured of any disease. This faithful servant carried the Child-God about. What innumerable graces, then, must have enriched the soul of this holy man from this contact? In Nazareth he was many years in company with Jesus and Mary; he conversed with them, prayed with them, shared their joys and their sorrows; every day and every moment he grew in grace and in virtue, enjoying without interruption the contemplation of Jesus, the Redeemer of the world. The eyes of the eternal Father were upon him, Jesus loved him with the affection of a son, our blessed Lady revered and obeyed him as one who had received authority from God; the angels were devoted to him as being privileged beyond any man on earth or even the angels in heaven.

Let us then honor this saint with our confidence and have a great devotion to him. 1. Let us keep his life always before our eyes and imitate his virtues. 2. Let us every day say some prayer in his honor. 3. Let us celebrate his feasts with great joy, and not only his feasts, but the whole month of March, which the Church devotes to him. 4. Let us keep a picture of the saint in our room, that we may be reminded to have recourse to him in all our necessities. 5. When we go to communion on his feast, or in fact at any time, let us invite St. Joseph to keep us company, that we may be inspired with a love of Our Lord who has come into our heart.

The Devotion to the Infant Jesus.

THE devotion to the Infant Jesus has been practised by all the saints and is attractive and useful to our spiritual life. It is a devotion especially adapted to young people, because it teaches the virtues which Our Lord practised in His childhood and which must be learned in early life.

The child is dear to Our Lord; once when He was asked "Who is the greater in the kingdom of God?" He hesitated not an instant; He did not look for the philosopher, nor the priest, nor even the apostles who had asked the question, but He showed them a little child. The little child is then in the mind of Our Lord the most beautiful object on earth or in heaven. Why? Because the love of Our Lord resides in that pure heart. Why not, then, early inform the child of God's predilection for it? Make the child give Our Lord great love in return, and impress on its mind a devotion to the sweet Infant Jesus.

We become by Baptism the branches of the heavenly vine Jesus, we are one with Him. He is the centre of our souls and we should be firmly united to Him.

St. Teresa, the foundress of the Reformed Carmelites, always carried about her a little statue of the Infant Jesus, and on her travels she would exhibit the little figure and the nuns would make their devotions before it. So great was their devotion and recollection that they appeared as though they were in their quiet cloister. It is related that on one occasion St. Teresa met on the stairs a beautiful child ; surprised, Teresa asked, " Where did you come from, my dear little child ? who are you ? " And the little one answered, " I will answer you when you have told me who you are." Teresa said, " I am Sister Teresa of Jesus," and the Infant replied, " I am Jesus of Sister Teresa," and suddenly disappeared.

The venerable Mother Ann of Jesus, sub-prioress under Teresa, also had a great devotion to the Child Jesus ; one day she received a little statue of the Infant Jesus, which she placed on the altar in the novitiate, and the simple devotion of one of the novices is thus told. " Every day I carried a bunch of flowers to the Infant Jesus, and I made the bouquet up in this wise : I put in some red flowers to express my desire for suffering and to do that which was hardest in community life ; I placed some white flowers in it to show my love of purity, and that the love of God would precede every other attachment ; I put in some yellow flowers to signify that I deeply regretted the offences against almighty God ; some blue flowers were there too, representing my tears for the conversion of sinners. Whenever I came with that bouquet, the divine Infant took it from my hand, and offered it to His eternal Father."

The Miraculous Statue of the Infant of Prague.

You have heard, my dear children, of the miraculous statue of the Infant of Prague; would it not be well in your devotions to take this as the symbol of your love for the Christ-Child, to make the little statue of the Infant of Prague a sensible, tangible means to keep the devotion alive in your practices of piety to the Infant Jesus ? You will certainly do so when you know its history, which is as follows : In 1628 Ferdinand II., emperor of Germany, founded a monastery of Discalced Carmelites in the city of Prague, the capital of Bohemia. After the erection of the monastery, the Princess Polyxene brought the Fathers a statue of the Infant Jesus, about a foot and a half high ; it represented the Infant Jesus standing, His right hand raised in benediction and in the left hand a golden globe, an image of the world. The face of the statue was very sweet and gracious; the dress and little cope was of gold, the work of the princess herself. In making the present, she said, "I give you, my dear Fathers, what I prize very

highly ; honor this statue, and you will want for
nothing."

The promise was verified to the letter. God
showered His blessings on the monastery. These
sons of St. Teresa placed the little statue in their
oratory, where it became at once the object of their
devotion, love, and confidence.

In 1681, a hostile army took possession of
Prague, the hands of the statue were broken off,
and the statue itself was thrown into a pile of rub-
bish. Here it lay for seven years, when it was discovered by Father Cyril, but on account of its
dress he did not notice that the hands of the Infant were gone. One day as he was praying before
the statue, he seemed to hear these words, " Have
compassion on me and I will have compassion on
you ; give me back my hands which have been
broken off, and I will give you sweet consolation
and peace ; the more you honor me, the more
graces will you receive." The priest was so poor
that he could not defray the necessary expense to
repair the statue, and he begged the Infant to send
some kind soul, who would pay for the work ; then
the voice said, " Place me at the entrance to the
sacristy, and some one will see me thus maimed,
and will have compassion on me." Soon a rich
man offered to restore the figure, and the Infant

Jesus richly rewarded him for his good deed. In 1638, the Blessed Virgin indicated the spot where the statue was to be permanently kept. Afterward a magnificent altar was built and the statue was placed in the tabernacle. Count Bernard, marquis of Bohemia, presented a handsome crown to the Infant of Prague; it was of gold covered with precious stones, and was placed on the head of the statue by the Archbishop of Prague, who at the end of the ceremony publicly kissed the feet of the little statue; after him followed the whole court. Up to the time of which we are speaking the Carmelites were the only ones who paid homage to the sacred image. In order to extend the devotion to the outside world, a chapel was built near the church, and in 1655 the Infant Jesus was carried there.

This little statue has been seen to change the expression of its face : sometimes it looks sweet, and at other times severe. The following incident is sworn to as true. A man, careless and indifferent about his religion, went to the chapel out of curiosity. Having heard so much of the Infant Jesus of Prague he looked at the statue, but he only saw the robe of the Child, the face and hands he could not see ; this made him think of himself and he said, "I must go to confession. I am sure that is the reason why I do not see the Infant Jesus." He went to confession and with great sorrow confessed his sins. When he came back he could see clearly the lovely face of the Infant Jesus, but soon it was covered again. "What is the reason of this disappearance?" he asked himself; and examining his conscience he found that in his haste to confess he had forgotten a very important thing. He again sought his confessor and after unburdening his conscience, the statue was revealed to him perfectly.

Once a thief wished to steal the rich vestments and precious stones of the statue; scarcely had he laid hold of them when he felt that he could not stir hand or foot; he was so frightened that the cold perspiration rolled off his pale face; he realized that God had thwarted his base designs. Filled with remorse, he prayed fervently and promised that he would lead a good life thenceforward. Immediately his strength returned, and he went directly to the Carmelite Fathers, to whom he related the fact.

The renown of this little statue spread far and wide, because many miracles were wrought by it. Every petition made to the Infant Jesus, if it were at all according to the will of God, was granted in all cases. From all parts of the world came letters begging for images of this holy Infant. They are made exactly like the original, are blessed by the Carmelite Fathers, and touched to the miraculous image. With the blessing go also the favors attributed to the original statue, as well as the promises made for it. It seems to be a fact that wherever the statue of the Infant of Prague is honored and kept, there too rests the blessing of God; God's graces in abundance, God's powerful protection.

In schools the devotion is loved by the children, and can be easily introduced for their spiritual benefit; they prize the little statue and pictures very much, and soon learn to have confidence in the kindness of the sweet Infant Jesus. The teacher, too, will find the devotion useful, for she can often refer to the Child Christ, and picture to the little ones how He practised a particular virtue; for example, silence, love of others, kindness to every one, love of truth and honesty, etc., etc.

The following prayer by Father Cyril to the Infant Jesus of Prague, is very beautiful, and you, my dear children, should repeat it often:

Jesus! unto Thee I flee,
Through Thy Mother praying Thee

In my need to succor me.
Truly, I believe of Thee
God Thou art with strength to shield me;
Full of trust I hope in Thee,
Thou Thy grace wilt give to me;
All my heart I give to Thee,
Therefore of my sins repent me;
From them breaking, I beseech Thee,
Jesus! from their bonds to free me.
Firm my purpose is to mend me,
Never more will I grieve Thee.
Wholly unto Thee I give me,
Patiently to suffer for Thee,
Thee to serve eternally,
And my neighbor like to me
I will love, for love of Thee.
Little Jesus, I beseech Thee
In my need to succor me,
That one day I may enjoy Thee,
Safe with Joseph, and with Mary,
And angels all, eternally.

The Child Jesus as God.

MY dear children, whose life have you been reading? Who is this wonderful Child whom we have adored with the shepherds and the Magi? It is the great God, the Second Person of the Blessed Trinity, who became man: it is the Son of God whom we acknowledge when in making the sign of the cross, we say, "In the name of the Father, and of the Son, and of the Holy Ghost." This Second Person, the Son of God, the eternal Word, who proceeds from the Father, became man. Therefore He was a Man-God, and though a weak Infant, unable to walk, to talk, or to defend Himself against the machinations of His enemies, still He was the God of heaven, all-powerful and all-wise. Or when we see Him a boy: good-hearted, noble, and generous, yet not working miracles as He did during His ministry; still He is God and could do wonderful things if He wished. Again, when we contemplate Him in His agony, dying in disgrace on the cross between two thieves, who were executed with Him, we would exclaim with the centurion, " Indeed this man was the Son of God." This is the same person who three days after His death rose glorious and immortal. We say in the Athanasian Creed, " This is the true faith, that we should believe and confess that Our Lord Jesus Christ is both God and man ; He is God begotten from the substance of His Father before the ages, and man made from the substance of His Mother and born in time."

See the sweet little Infant Jesus held out towards you by His blessed Mother ; He smiles on you because you love Him, and because you wish to be good : what does all this endearment mean, except the love of God for us ? That Heart of Jesus invites us to come to Him. He is our rightful Master, because He is our God ; and oh, what a kind and tender Master we would find in Him, if we would go to Him ! This little Child is with the Father and the Holy Ghost, the one true God in heaven, undivided from the Blessed Trinity, and on earth, in the form of a babe. The Child Jesus is the centre of all the works of God, because from Him have emanated all creatures; angels and men, the universe, the earth, and all things have come forth at His command, and are bound to Him by being preserved in existence by His will. How great a child He is then that has done such wonderful things ; for there is no power, save the omnipotence of God alone, that can create !

In Jesus there are two natures : the divine, which always was and which is the nature of God, and the human, which He took from the Blessed Virgin Mary ; but there is but one person, the sacred person of Jesus Christ, and it is because there is only one person in Jesus that Mary is the true Mother of God. Therefore, Mary is indeed worthy of our love, our respect, and our honor, because she has given us the sacred humanity of Jesus. As Mary sits enthroned on the humble rock in the cave of Bethlehem, holding towards us the Infant Jesus, she is greater than the arch-angels who are supposed to be the highest crea-tures of God's power, because she is their queen. We can go to her with great confidence, and we should love her, too, for she is so good, so affable, so kind, and so loving.

Furthermore there are other signs of the divin-ity of this Child Jesus : in His subsequent life He had to announce Himself and to declare Himself, and He did so ; He always maintained that He was the Son of God ; the Jews crucified Him be-cause He said He was the Son of God, and they said He blasphemed, and He undoubtedly would have been guilty of blasphemy had He not been really and truly the Son of God. St. Peter was asked by Our Lord Himself, "Whom do you say that I am?" and Peter answered, "Thou art Christ, the Son of the living God." The centurion who pierced with a lance the side of Our Lord hanging on the cross, when he saw the dreadful things that happened, the darkness that spread over the world, the spirits of departed men going about, the earthquakes that rent the rocks, said, "Indeed, this man was the Son of God."

God the Father spoke twice in an audible voice: once at Christ's baptism and again at His transfiguration on Mount Thabor, "This is My beloved Son in whom I am well pleased; hear ye Him."

After his conversion, Paul, the persecutor of Our Lord, said openly before the Jews, that Jesus was over all things, God: blessed forever, in whom dwelleth the fulness of the Godhead corporally: that every knee should bow before Him in heaven, on earth, and in hell.

"Jesus Christ judges as a God, punishes as a God, rewards as a God, exacts obedience as a God, and claims our love above all things. The divinity of Christ is the corner-stone of our faith, our Christianity, of our holy Mother the Church. In Him is centred all our hope and confidence for our future glory. He is the object of our love and adoration in the humble crib, in His glorious life, in His death on the cross, in the Blessed Sacrament on our altars, and sitting in heaven at the right hand of God the Father" (Card. Gibbons).

Oft as Thee, my Infant Saviour,
  In Thy Mother's arms I view,
Straight a thousand thrilling raptures
  Overflow my heart anew.

Happy Babe! and happy Mother!
  Oh, how great your bliss must be!
Each enfolded in the other,
  Sipping pure felicity!

Lowly Jesus! gentle Brother,
  How I wish a smile from Thee,
Meant for Thy immortal Mother,
  Only might alight on me !
                    —*Edward Caswall.*

The Sacred Heart of the Infant Jesus.

THERE is one great devotion to Our Lord of
which children should think and which they
should practise. Among Catholics there is the devotion to the Sacred Heart of Our Lord, that has
reference not only to Him in His public life, but
all through His lifetime. We admire the goodness
of the Heart of Our Lord in His public career, for
He never passed human misery without relieving
it ; He never saw infirmity without His kind
Heart being impelled to cure it. He loved humanity to such a degree that He said, " My delight is
to be with the children of men." His Heart was
the same when He was a child, and His words :
" Suffer the little children to come unto Me, for
of such is the kingdom of God," apply to Him as
a child as well as when He was grown to man's
estate, for as a child He loved children and never
so enjoyed His childhood games and sports as
when with other children. So it is with the Child
Jesus. His Heart is ever open to receive little
ones, and we are sure to please Him when we adore

and love His infant Heart. You can, therefore, my dear little children, do as older people do, and practise a simple devotion to the Sacred Heart of the Infant Jesus.

There was a good and very pious nun, the Blessed Margaret Mary, at Paray-le-Monial, in France, to whom Our Lord appeared and said, "Behold, this Heart which has so loved men that it has spared nothing, even to exhausting and consuming itself, in order to testify its love. In return, I receive from the greater part only ingratitude, by their irreverence and sacrilege, and by the coldness and contempt they have for Me in this sacrament of love. And what is most painful to Me," added Our Saviour in a tone that went to the Sister's heart, "is that they are hearts consecrated to Me." Then He commanded her to have established in the Church a particular feast to honor His Sacred Heart. "It is for this reason that I ask thee that the first Friday after the octave of the Blessed Sacrament be appropriated to a special feast, to honor My Heart by communicating on that day, and making reparation for the indignity that it has received. And I promise that My Heart shall dilate to pour out abundantly the influences of its love on all that will render it this honor, or procure its being rendered."

Though some children may not have made their first communion and hence cannot receive the Blessed Eucharist, still they can practise a part of the devotion. They can make the morning offering, they can say their little decade of the rosary, they can be present at the exposition of the Blessed Sacrament and adore Jesus there.

Through the zeal of the good Jesuit Fathers the devotion to the Sacred Heart of Jesus has been extended to the schools and a little league called the Apostleship of Study has been formed to bring children to a knowledge of the Heart of Jesus, and to give them the opportunity of approaching more closely the Sacred Heart of Our Lord. The object and aim of the league in schools is to cultivate in the hearts of our children a love for the Pope, and a love for the Church, to be shown by an aversion to secret societies; a love for our holy religion, to be shown by frequent approach to the sacraments; finally, a love for that study and training which are to make the pupils of Catholic schools ornaments to their religion and country, and benefactors to their people. It is wonderful how children appreciate this little confidence in their power of doing some good. In order to consecrate school life in a special way to the Sacred Heart of Jesus, members of the Apostleship of

Study should offer every day : 1. An hour of study; 2. An hour of silence; 3. An hour of recreation : the three chief duties of a school-day.

By this consecration of school-life to the Heart of Jesus, the ordinary routine of the classroom and playground may be offered like a prayer, either to intercede for the welfare of the Sovereign Pontiff, or to thank God for His consolations and triumphs.

The Child Jesus in the Blessed Sacrament.

WE think, my dear children, that since Jesus has gone from us, we have no opportunity of personally showing our respect, our love, and our gratitude to Him. We say to ourselves, Jesus ascended into heaven on Ascension Day, and sits at the right hand of God the Father, and we cannot reach Him, except as we reach the saints, by our prayers. But the Lord Jesus is not gone out of this world ; He did not go back to the Father leaving us alone. No ; He is here amongst us in the adorable Sacrament of the Altar as really and as truly as when He was on earth. This is what the Church teaches. Now let us see what is to be believed as regards Christ's presence, and what is the consequence of this belief.

The Church teaches that Jesus is present in the Holy Eucharist, really and truly, that His body and soul as well as His divinity are there under the form of bread and wine. It is therefore a part of our faith that Jesus is present with us, that we can go to Him, visit Him, and love Him ; He is not

a dead Lord, but a living God, and we can have a
personal interview with Him. My dear children,
early in life we are taught this truth, but how
little do we realize it ! What should be the consequence of believing that Jesus Christ is present on
our altars ? I should think if we were thoroughly
and intimately persuaded of it our churches would
be considered privileged places, they would never
be empty, we would go there for every necessity,
because we know that there we could obtain all we
need from the sweet Heart of Jesus ; we would
stay in church, thinking of Jesus, adoring Him
and loving Him ; we would bring to our altars all
that we have, even the most precious ; we would
have churches as magnificent as kings' palaces, and
altars of gold and precious stones ; we would have
a number of candles constantly burning to show
our faith and attention to Our Lord, nor would we
wish to tear ourselves from Him. There on the
altar is the throne of God, as we read it described
in the Apocalypse, when St. John was called to
look at the wonderful vision of the reality of
heaven.

"There was a throne set in heaven, and upon
the throne One sitting. And He that sat, was to
the sight like the jasper and the sardine-stone: and
there was a rainbow round about the throne, in

sight like unto an emerald. And round about the throne were four and twenty seats : and upon the seats four and twenty ancients sitting, clothed in white garments, and on their heads were crowns of gold : And from the throne proceeded lightnings, and voices, and thunders : and there were seven lamps burning before the throne, which are the seven spirits of God. And in the sight of the throne was as it were a sea of glass like to crystal : and the four and twenty ancients fell down before Him that sitteth on the throne, and adored Him that liveth forever and ever, and cast their crowns before the throne, saying : Thou art worthy, O Lord our God, to receive glory and honor and power : because Thou hast created all things, and for Thy will they were, and have been created."

Such is the invisible throne of Jesus on the altar, where Our Saviour is hidden under the veil of bread and wine. Jesus hides His majesty, for we are not yet ready for the glory of heaven which was seen by St. John. Jesus in the Holy Eucharist is surrounded by the same grandeur as He is in heaven. In that wonderful sacrament we have the Child Jesus always amongst us ; we are on our knees before the Infant God, when we kneel before His tabernacle ; we are at the feet of the same

Infant God who lay in Mary's arms on that first Christmas night ; the same eyes are looking at us, with a smile of welcome lighting up His face. Oh, what happiness ! Why need we envy the shepherds and Magi ? We are as blessed as they were. We see Him, we adore Him, we can receive Him as fully and as entirely as they saw Him in the mystery of His incarnation in that poor cave. The priest stands guard over the Lord Jesus in the Holy Eucharist ; he presents Him to us in holy communion, carries Him to us in the Viaticum, and blesses us with Him in benediction.

The light which burns day and night before the Blessed Sacrament is like a star which shines for us as the Star of Bethlehem did for the Magi, inviting us to come to the altar and adore the Lord God ; that light speaks to us and tells us that the divine Infant is to be found in that lowly tabernacle ; it indicates the very spot and twinkles to us a welcome at that throne. How respectful, my dear children, you ought to be in church in the presence of Our Lord ; there you ought to pray and fix your mind on God ; you should not look about you at the people, nor should you talk to your companions. Like the angels you should be attentive to God's presence, for so impressed are they with a knowledge of God's greatness that they are continually in profound adoration before Him. There is no greater treasure than the divine Child in the Blessed Sacrament. Our entire religious life without the Blessed Sacrament would be an empty shell. In every church the most conspicuous object is the altar on which the holy sacrifice is offered, and where the Blessed Sacrament is kept. Let us cherish a constant and a fervent desire for this great and sublime mystery, and let us cultivate, with a meek and humble heart, a better knowledge and a greater love of the divine Child in the Most Blessed Sacrament.

> Sweet Jesus! by this Sacrament of Love
> All gross affections from my heart remove;
> Let but Thy loving-kindness linger there,
> Preserved by grace and perfected by prayer;
> And let me to my neighbor strive to be
> As mild and gentle as Thou art with me.
> Take Thou the guidance of my whole career,
> That to displease Thee be my only fear;
> Give me that peace the world can never give,
> And in Thy loving presence let me live.
> Ah! show me always, Lord, Thy holy will,
> And to each troubled thought say, " *Peace, be still!* "

LAUDATE PUERI DOMINUM

The Child Jesus in the Hearts of Little Ones.

THE divine Infant should be in our souls by our love of Jesus, by our devotion to Our Lord, and by the virtues of humility and poverty which we should continue to practise until this life is over and we depart to the other world in the company of Jesus. With what a great desire Our Lord wished to be born in our hearts! the whole intention of Christ's incarnation was to be born in us. By the sacraments of the Church this is realized and perpetuated. In Baptism, the sacrament of infancy, the sacrament at the beginning of the spiritual life, Our Lord is first born in our heart; He makes it His habitation. By the presence of God a character is impressed on that soul, it is made the temple of the Holy Ghost. Our Lord was there and is there, as Jacob said when he had those sublime visions in the desert, and went and consecrated a stone to mark the sacred place. It is the same with our souls: they have been visited by God, who has consecrated them as His temples, and has placed His seal upon them. We are by

Baptism branches of the great vine, Jesus Our Lord ; we are one with Him ; He is the root and trunk and we are the shoots engrafted upon it. My dear little children, what wonderful creatures you are, for your bodies are the sanctuaries of the Holy of holies in which only God should be enthroned, in which the King of angels should dwell. We can drive out God from that soul and put the devil in His place ; but what an exchange that would be ! the devil in hell should never have power over us ; that is the reason that only God can live in the soul of a Christian ; if any other master obtain possession of it, it is a desecration of the temple of God.

Let us reproduce in our hearts the life of Christ; the young come nearest to the life which Jesus led and which He desires us to lead. The life of Christ must be reproduced in innumerable ways ; it must be reproduced in the heart of every child as it plays on the street, studies in school, obeys its mother in the home, prays, and adores God in church. That life of Christ should be reproduced by the merchant in doing justice to all ; keeping God before His eyes ; using the world as if he were not using it ; poor in spirit, yet laboring to gather riches ; with charity for the poor, generosity to the Church, and so continuing his Christ-like life until he is called to his eternal reward. This life has to be reproduced in the father and mother of the family, in the son and daughter, in all souls that live in this world; as Faber says: "Then the life of a good Christian is like a grand heavenly recitation, which Providence itself pronounces as the years go on with a sort of dramatic silence. Each single human life in the world amounts to nothing less than a private revelation of God, but when a man is living in a state of grace, this life becomes still more wonderful because it is supernatural."

> Dear Jesus, keep us in Thy Heart!
>   Take our cold hearts away,
> Or make our hearts more like to Thine,
>   More pure and meek each day.
> Ah! yes, e'en in this sinful world
>   This is the better part:
> What shall it be when safe for aye,
>   Lord, in Thy Sacred Heart?

Jesus the Model of Purity.

God, my dear children, is sanctity itself. Whatever is the purest and noblest is in comparison to His splendor as insignificant as the shadow is to the light of the sun. The bright angels and the purified saints feel the splendor and immensity of God so much that their continual song is " Holy, holy, holy is the Lord our God. The heavens and the earth are full of His glory."

Jesus Christ, the only Son of God the Father, is perfectly equal to Him in sanctity, only He lowered Himself to become man and to expiate our sins ; He too must be pure and free from sin as regards His body. He knew sin only as far as He wished to atone for it. When the Jews were persecuting Him and accusing Him, He could frankly ask them, " Which of you can convict Me of sin ? " At your age, my dear children, the good Infant Jesus hid his inimitable sanctity in the holy house of Nazareth and under a humble exterior. We know from the few words of the Gospel that all

were struck with the growth of this Youth in
the wisdom of God. Yes, indeed, this Child
was the object of the happiness of God the
Father ; He was the Temple of the Holy Trinity
in its literal sense. All who came in contact with
Him no doubt felt themselves purified by His presence; they felt that they were so inferior to this
Child in sanctity they naturally searched their
hearts to find their defects and so to correct themselves.

Jesus in His childhood had none of the defects
of which youth in general is guilty ; nothing of
that pride or sensuality so often seen in young
men; no caprices or stubbornness; no seeking for
comfort or satisfaction of the appetites ; He never
got angry and played cruel tricks. The sanctity
of Christ at this time of His life must have shone
forth so distinctly and at the same time so inde-
scribably that all would be struck by it and still
would not be able to say that it made Him singular ; He was indeed the most beautiful of the
children of men. His forehead shines with a bright
halo, His eyes, habitually cast down in modesty,
frequently light up with a supernatural brightness
and kindness. About His lips plays a smile which
at once consoles and attracts. His clothes are simple, but neat and becoming; everything about this

holy Youth inspires the love of virtue and all become better for being near Him.

This very goodness and graciousness will be ap-
parent also in those young people who try to imitate Our Lord in His youth : for that holy example will show itself in their every act. .

Once a pious youth having served at the altar,
and his clothes smelling of incense, said to his
mother, "Do I not smell as if I had been with
the good God ?" That is what we understand
when we hear that people are the odor of Jesus
Christ ; it issues from the heart of a well-disposed
Christian, and its edifying effect spreads among
those who come in contact with it.

Confide the precious treasure of innocence to the
Child Jesus and co-operate with the grace given
you to preserve it from all profanation. Hide, as
did your Child-Master, your sanctity in the interior
of your house, in the house of God ; do not expose
it to the chance of being damaged by the devil
or the evil example of a wicked world. Open not
your eyes to the vanities of the world nor to the
scandals in it. Forget not that you are continually
under the eye of God ; often call on Him to assist
you in this struggle. Your body and your soul
belong to God, because they have been consecrated
to Him in baptism : let no one claim anything of

God's property ; you are more precious and more holy than the golden vessels of the altar which only the priest should touch.

According to the example of the Child Jesus remain always under the guardianship of Mary immaculate and of St. Joseph the father and protector of virgins. Be one of those who belong to the ranks of the pure, virginal Christian youth. How beautiful is the chaste generation of hearts where virtue reigns ; that virtue is undying, God preserves it, the angels venerate it, and man is justly proud of it.

That beautiful virtue of purity finds a congenial soil in the deep valley of retirement ; there it grows under the helping grace of heaven ; some time it will be transplanted to the garden of God in paradise, where it will flourish for all eternity. The Child Jesus is the immaculate lily, and He invites us to love that spot where the lilies grow, for He tells us that He rejoices to walk among the lilies. You will be received under His white banner only if you are dressed in purest white, for you have preserved your innocence. Purity is then a most inestimable treasure. When a good Catholic youth is pure, Jesus Christ wants that youth for His friend and companion. Once when St. Stanislaus Kostka was lying on his sick-bed Mary brought her divine Son, as a little child, and placed Him in his arms, and Jesus was glad to remain an instant on the bosom of this saint. Our Lord fills with generous gifts of grace that young person who is in a state of grace and destines him for great things to His honor in this world. Even the wickedest worldlings are forced to acknowledge that the young man who can preserve his purity is an excellent young man and there is nothing in all the gay world to compare with him. This is certain, that a youth who reaches twenty or twenty-one and has not lost his purity is the most generous, the best, the most attractive, the most amiable person. The Church does not hesitate to say that a young man who is virtuous is an angel. In pictures we see a lily in the hands of St. Stanislaus, John Berchmans, and Aloysius Gonzaga, and these the Church calls angelic youths. But if the lily is the most beautiful of flowers, it is also a most delicate one. In order to bring it to its greatest glory it must be looked after carefully and be preserved from every rough treatment, away from dirt and dust ; it grows best far from the high-road, near the borders of a stream, surrounded by thorns. Your soul, my dear children, ornamented with purity and holiness by Baptism, needs just as much care as a beautiful lily. Keep your soul constantly in the presence of God by fervent prayer : then she will be out of the reach of the mud of the highway. Shut your eyes to all evil curiosity : guard your looks. Many is the youth that has fallen from grace by careless looks. St. Aloysius Gonzaga never raised his eyes to a woman, not even to his mother: St. Berchmans was so modest that no one could ever detect him in a fault of the eyes.

Abhor all intimacy that leads to sin, every evil word, or word of double meaning. St. Stanislaus actually fainted when an impure word was uttered in his presence. When St. Berchmans came among his companions, they said at once, " Here is the angel," and their conversation, if bad, was dropped at once. All the young saints of whom we know confided their purity to the Blessed Virgin by frequent communions. In the Holy Eucharist are found all the means to defend our soul against every temptation ; it is the bread of angels and the wine that begets virgins. A young man leaving the service of a man where many scandalous things were going on, said to his confessor : " I was really bad at first, but since I go frequently to holy communion I do not even feel temptations : and when these temptations were thrust on me at my place of business I became so disgusted that I left it."

You certainly wish to be pure, my dear children; go then frequently to the banquet of the angels; you will obtain your wish to remain pure, to hate impurity, and to fly every occasion of a temptation. You will feel a disgust at this filthy vice of impurity and will hate the place where it is practised.

Jesus at Prayer.

"THE continual prayer of a just man availeth much" (James v. 16).

The first duty of youth is to love God and to learn to be submissive to His law. We all are servants of God, or at least that is our natural condition, and we would love Him if we were in the state in which God intended us to be, but from which we strayed by the sin of our first parents. The first and principal duty of every Christian is to hold himself firmly in that condition; nothing will do it for him but prayer; prayer raises our souls towards heaven from the things of this world.

By our depraved nature we have been led into sin. The mission of Jesus Our Lord on this earth was to re-establish our natural relations with God; from His Sacred Heart there arose constantly the incense of prayer to His Father. The Child Jesus had His hours of prayer, and Mary and Joseph joined in fervor with Him.

What a beautiful picture is that of the Child

Jesus in prayer ! A God-man, a child praying for us. His body is on earth, but His soul is in heaven in prayer.

The divine Child is prostrated before the divine majesty of His heavenly Father. Sometimes His hands are joined, His eyes cast down, His head inclined; He humbles Himself. At times tears course down His cheeks to obtain pardon for our sins ; at times His arms are extended towards heaven and His eyes raised. Joseph and Mary are rapt in ecstasy; the angels, invisible to the eyes of men, unite with them. This same, my dear children, you also must do. Go on your knees, join your hands, shut your eyes to the world, and pray with Jesus, Mary and Joseph.

When St. Aloysius Gonzaga was a child he could pray for a full hour without a distraction. We should pray in the same manner. We can do it by asking the favor of God's grace.

The Child Jesus never lost sight of His heavenly Father ; He walked continually in His presence. Even at His work His soul was in constant communion with heaven. His first thoughts at waking were sanctified by directing them to God, and at night He fell asleep with the thought of God on His mind.

Do we send up our first thoughts to God who

has preserved us during the night and given us another day ? Do we place our whole being in the hands of God before retiring, and when the striking of the clock reminds us that we are approaching eternity ? Do we pray before and after our meals, our studies, our recreations, and the various exercises of the day ? And yet constant prayer is necessary if we wish to save our souls. Jesus tells us to pray always and never cease praying. In order to continue His prayer Jesus has hidden Himself in the tabernacle on our altars.

We see so many young people go astray and fall into sin, because they pray badly. Prayer is the breath of the soul. When the body no longer breathes it is dead ; in the same way if we cease to pray we are fast nearing the death of our soul. Prayer is a sign of spiritual health. St. Francis de Sales says if you pray well you are in good spiritual health. When John Berchmans assisted at Mass people used to gather to see him pray, and were so edified by his actions that they would say, " He is an angel."

St. Aloysius Gonzaga was so engrossed in prayer that it was with difficulty that he could be called from it. Octave de Ravinel, a young Jesuit, prayed so well and so often that in his last sickness he said to the doctor who forbade him to speak, that

he was " very glad of it, for it will give me time
to think uninterruptedly of Our Lord." When
death was coming on he was heard repeating, " O
Jesus, I love Thee; Jesus, I love Thee with all my
soul."

You, my children, can also accustom yourselves to such habitual prayer ; be encouraged to
it by the command of Jesus and the good examples
we have cited. Do not pray merely with your
lips as the Jews did who were reproached by God,
whilst their heart was far from Him. Go to Mass
and to the Church services, as did the Child Jesus,
who, according to the law of Moses, went to the
Temple and celebrated the feasts.

Youth is considered the springtime of life ;
now in the spring the sun shines on the plants and
trees so brightly and so warm that the flowers blossom in abundance, the birds sing more gayly, and
all nature seems to revive after a long and dreary
winter. Piety and prayer are the beautiful sun of
your youthful life, and under its benign influence
the virtues ought to blossom and bear fruit for
after years. Love prayer then, dear children, be
pious, induce your parents to invite you to prayer;
they will join you and will themselves feel the
beneficent influence of this practical exercise of
your religion.

Piety is useful to all and the benefits of the present life as well as those of the future are promised us by means of it.

The Humility of the Child Jesus.

WHEN He was your age, my dear children, Our Lord went to work with His foster-father St. Joseph, and walked modestly through the streets of the little village of Nazareth. He was dressed in a clean, but rough dress, carried heavy pieces of wood on His shoulders, and in His hands was a rude basket in which were carpenter's tools. The people of the village did not know who this Child was, but neighbors and acquaintances pointed Him out to the other youths of the place as a perfect model of a good boy, and they said to one another, "That is the little Carpenter and His father going to their day's work." And perfectly well did they know them, for in the after life of Jesus they refused to believe in Him, because He was the carpenter's son, and they did not know in what school He had learned all the heavenly wisdom which He taught. Still they knew Him not, because they could only see the exterior, which was no different from that of other youths, except that He was so good and no fault could be found in Him. Jesus

217

was, however, happy to live thus unknown among these people. We learn from this the virtue of humility, and following Our Lord's example we should strive to be gentle and humble of heart.

Pride is always a detestable vice, but is especially abominable in young people. Let us also learn to be humble because it is such a becoming virtue, necessary not only in our youth, but throughout life. But how are we to acquire that virtue ? The whole may be summed up in a few words, namely, a youth practises this virtue when he remains quiet and content in the station he has inherited from his parents; when he does not wish to have more made of him than he is, a poor creature that has to be sustained in existence by a perpetual miracle of God's power, one that is full of faults and capable of doing anything wicked. Of ourselves we are nothing ; we have nothing on which to pride ourselves ; neither our talents, nor our good qualities, nor our genius, nor our ancestors ought to be a source of pride to us, for all these are gifts from God ; and, because we have in many things been at fault, we deserve really to be despised by every one.

A young man who is proud is in reality a liar, for he wants to appear what he is not and acts continually as if he wanted to make others believe in his excellence. To preserve us from this ridiculous pride or to cure us of it Our Lord hides His infinite majesty and appears in the modest, but lowly, garb of a workman. At His age He had mastered all science; He certainly could have held the highest place in the most brilliant school ; He would have put to shame the most learned teacher. Once when He appeared among the doctors He astonished them, and we see the extraordinary spectacle of a child teaching the learned men of His day. But in order to give glory to God His Father and to expiate your pride and teach you humility, Jesus condemned Himself to a long silence in His youth, up to His thirtieth year, and He only preached during three years of His life. Had this holy Child been treated as He deserved, He should have wielded a sceptre of power, worn a regal crown, and been dressed in purple. But what should we think of a God who was covered with the vanities of this world, and what example would He have given to the youth of all times ! Youth is inclined to wear good clothes, to follow the fashions of the world, and to draw the attention of every one to itself. On the contrary, the Son of the most humble Virgin desired to be the most humble youth on earth. He received only the education of the poor ; He chose only the sons

of poor people for His companions. He appeared
to need to learn the trade of a carpenter as if He
could neither read nor write.

Pray then to this divine Child Jesus of Nazareth
to obtain for you the grace to be humble. Abhor
the ridiculous pretensions of your little vanities.
Pride created hell and has never ceased to send
souls to it. Humility is so natural to youth that
Our Lord once publicly said, " Unless you become
as little children, you shall not enter into the kingdom of heaven." Young saints, your patrons, following the Child Jesus, have distinguished themselves by their humility.

St. Aloysius Gonzaga was of princely extrac-
tion : he might with all propriety have dressed in
the richest and most fashionable manner, but he
never wore rich clothing nor carried jewelry. One
day, to let people see how little he cared for the
consideration of the fashionable world, he went to
the celebration of a feast in a very simple dress,
on a horse which was put to shame by the animals
which his companions rode. Nothing gave our
young saint so much pain as to hear himself praised.
Like St. Augustine, he considered praise a real
punishment. At an examination from which he
came with great distinction, he would not listen
to praise. He was very much saddened when he

was told how great was his rank and the distinction of his family. The same can be said of St. John Berchmans. When he was praised he always reminded people of the fact that he was the son of a poor workman ; he considered that the praises of man made little difference to him in the presence of God. He used to say, " I must not forget what I have been ; that I am nothing but an ulcer from which comes corruption."

We read lately of a young man who died at the age of nineteen and was declared venerable by the Holy Father, Pope Leo XIII. This youth was never known to have committed a fault. But he was only a beggar who went about the streets of Naples. He was sickly, dressed in rags, emaciated by disease, and his sole possession was a little book, the Office of the Blessed Virgin, and a pair of beads. However, his humility, his resignation, gave him such a joyful countenance that everybody said " he is an angel," but he said, " I am but a poor sinner, and if I still have confidence in God, it is because my Saviour came into this world not for the just, but for sinners." Often from humility he remained silent and prayed ; he did not like to be noticed, nor to speak of himself. So many miracles have occurred at his tomb that the Church, guided by God, is about to place him on its altars and recommend him as the patron of all young apprentices.

Such is the humility, my dear children, of the young saints of God. The world may criticise them, and hate such examples of humility, but God has crowned them with glory and the Church praises their virtue before the whole world.

This is certain and we are assured of it by the sacred Scriptures, that our true glory, our great glory, is to be a disciple of the humble Jesus.

The Obedience of the Child Jesus.

DISOBEDIENCE dug the depths of hell. The devil was the first one that disobeyed God, and for him and his followers hell was created. Ever since then the devil seeks to make us keep up the disobedience which he began against God ; he rebelled and was banished from heaven : in revenge he wishes to make us all disobedient, that we, too, will go to hell with him. Too often, indeed, does he succeed in gaining us over to his rebellion. Our first parents disobeyed God at the instigation of Satan, and they were sent out of paradise.

Young people of bad dispositions, who have no heart, are always disobedient. They are ignorant, weak creatures, they want to be their own masters, they know better than any one else. How foolish this is ! And they can hardly be convinced of their wrong-doing. Our Lord while a youth preached quite a different kind of life. Great were the virtues which for thirty years He practised in Nazareth, and still nothing is said of them all, not one is mentioned, except this one virtue: " He was subject to them." The Holy Scriptures know the value of obedience, and have distinguished it accordingly.

Jesus was obedient. That is a great mystery indeed. Jesus the Child, the great God, who knows all, who must be obeyed, who cannot be mistaken because He is infinitely wise, obeys Joseph and Mary who, at best, were only creatures with the limited minds of creatures. But Our Lord obeys as a child ; and you will see Him obey when He is a grown man, and that He is not ashamed to be subject to the will of His Mother.

What a great honor would it be to us if ours was that one distinction, that we were obedient ; that whatever order was given it was immediately obeyed ; that even anticipating the wishes of our parents and masters we should do what is to be done, so as to spare them the trouble of giving the order. Such good youths Our Lord will certainly love ; He will show them to His heavenly Father and say, " Here is My brother in the flesh, for he has no other desire than to obey your law." The angels themselves will applaud your obedience, for they will sing your praises, " Peace and happiness to the youth who obeys with good will." Great merit for all eternity you will of course gain by obedience.

In order that your obedience may be still more
meritorious it must be a Christian virtue : not
impelled by a mere human motive ; we must practise the virtue in reference to God from a supernatural motive. You obey your superiors because
they are the representatives of God on earth. Then
let your obedience be prompt, very willing, without a murmur, with a good heart, and all for God.

Here is a young reprobate who stands up boldly
and says : " I know what I'm about ; I obey God,
that's all ; I take no orders from any one."

God does not command us in person in everything. He delegates others who are to do that
work for Him ; these are called our superiors.
Hence when a young man has any sense he will
be respectful to his superior, because in him he sees
a representative of the authority of God, and
usually God's orders are given to us by our superiors. Angels are represented as having wings.
Why ? What do wings mean ? Wings represent
the prompt, willing, quick reception of the will of
God and the executing of it. Mary called herself
the handmaid of the Lord. Therefore a good
young man above all else will be obedient : it will
be the growth of his soul and body to obey the
will of God.

An obedient youth has no dangers to fear ; he

triumphs over temptations. The sacred Scriptures tell us that " An obedient man shall speak of victory."

By order of his superior a lay Brother of an African mission had to go to a station afar off. At nightfall he reached a forest in which he knew ferocious wild beasts were prowling about. Suddenly an enormous lion came along and was about to pounce on him, when the Brother with great coolness said, " Hold on, I'm here by order of my superiors ; you must not touch me ; let me go my way." We are told that the savage beast walked away as if ashamed of itself for having made such a mistake as to attack a man who was doing his duty. In obedience, at least at your time of life, my dear children, is salvation not only for life, but for eternity.

Jesus obeyed even unto death. He has declared that in His disciples He expected the great virtue of obedience. In the lives of the saints there are magnificent examples of obedience. In the year 1613 a young religious, Jean Pinto, died. At the end of his religious life, whilst he was praying, Jesus appeared to him. The holy religious asked of Jesus as a favor that before his death he might be granted the grace of possessing the perfection of the virtues of charity and chastity. " What ? "

said Our Lord in return, with a reproachful tone, "What, Jean, you do not ask for the virtue of obedience?" Then the servant of God quickly threw himself at the feet of Jesus and begged the virtue of obedience, and for the days still left to him on this earth he was the most perfect model of obedience.

For your own good and to bring joy to the Heart of Jesus, resist the ordinary obstinacy and pride of most young men, who are too proud to be told anything. Obedience is required of us in whatever position we may find ourselves in life. There is no need to take up time to prove this, but grown people, of years of experience, have found that no one is exempt from obedience.

Be kind to those who are your superiors, make their task easy by your docility and amiability, take their advice and their counsel in good part, and when they have to correct you see that they do not find you unwilling, stubborn, or hard to manage. Be an obedient child of the Church of God on earth, a good child of the holy Roman Catholic Church; obey her precepts, learn her teachings; she is infallible; be not ashamed to go to church, to say your prayers, and to show that you are a good young man, even though your companions laugh at you.

Honor the priests of the Church, for by them are dispensed the mysteries of the house of God.

Obey the laws of the land. Let us not break the law even though we think it affects our personal liberty. Let us not gamble nor go to gambling dens, because it is against the law of the country. Let the same principle guide us in all things.

"Render to Cæsar the things that are Cæsar's, and to God the things that are God's." But if a law should be bad, or unjust, be bold enough to denounce it as the martyrs of the early Church did, and as the apostles did who said, "We ought to obey God rather than men."

Jesus the Model of Industry.

JESUS is the Son of God and a descendant of the kings of Israel. The Jews could not but know that He was of the royal house of David, for they had seen Joseph and Mary depart at the command of Cæsar Augustus to be enrolled in the royal city of Bethlehem. Still we never find that Christ prided Himself on the title. He was known in His youth as the carpenter's son and helper.

The calling of an honest working man is an honorable one, and not to be despised. At the head of the working men, as their patron, is Jesus Christ Our Lord, the Son of God, God Himself. From His early childhood He learned the use of tools.

Dear children, if you are inclined to do nothing, and to pass your time idly; if you are vexed that you have to study or even to work in your youth, take your books or your tools to Nazareth to the carpenter shop of Joseph. There you will find the Child Jesus passing the greater part of His time in useful occupation for the purpose of

helping to gain a livelihood : and there He prepared Himself for thirty years for the great work
of His life, the preaching of the Gospel, and,
finally, for the great sacrifice of Himself on the
cross.

Enter that place with respect and adore God the
Laborer. His holy house is known to us ; angels
have taken it up and transported it to Loretto, to
remove it from the profanation of the Mohamme-
dans who are now dominant in the Holy Land.
The house was among the poorest in Nazareth, it
was lost among them, for there was nothing dis-
tinctive in it; like the others it was built of a red
limestone ; it had a vaulted roof, on which the
family might take the air at certain times of the
day and also assemble for prayer in common.
Fig trees, olive trees, and oranges set it off beauti-
fully, however.

But what a miserable palace for the King of
kings ! It was a house with a door towards the
road, the rear abutted against the natural rock,
and it was divided into three rooms. At the entrance was a room used as a workshop : a carpenter's bench was the most conspicuous article of
furniture, along the walls were hung saws and
squares, here and there lay planes, on the floor
were shavings and pieces of wood. The next room

was a kitchen and a sitting-room ; strangers were
not admitted there ; only relatives and intimate
acquaintances entered there. In this chamber it
is said that the archangel Gabriel visited Mary
to announce to her the will of God in her behalf,
that she should become the Mother of God. Beyond this spot the house stood against a cave
which, it is said, was the abode of the Child Jesus
and to which He retired in prayer. Such was the
home of this great Being whom the angels adore
and before whom they veil their faces in adoration. We ought to blush before Jesus when we
are opposed to work because we think ourselves
above it.

What was the work of the divine Infant Jesus
when He grew to a greater strength? Joseph made
wooden yokes for oxen, ploughs, boxes, trunks, and
ladders. Carpentry, at that time in Nazareth, was
a very small business ; houses were built of stone,
and the roofs were vaulted and needed no wood ;
only the furniture of the house was made by the
carpenter. This was the work of Jesus also, and
for thirty years He continued it. He gained His
livelihood by the sweat of His brow in fact; though
He was the almighty God who created the world
and could make what He wanted at His command.
During all those years He held His divinity cap-

tive and stripped it of all power ; He never called upon it to help Him in His temporal necessities. Whilst young men generally dislike work, Our Saviour gave us to understand how important faithful and continuous work is.

Man is born for work as the bird is for flight. As soon as Adam was created and placed in paradise God gave it to him to work in, regulate, and even beautify by the labor of his hands. It was of course a pleasant occupation, still it was work. Idleness is therefore in opposition to the will of God. Since sin came into the world labor has ceased to be a pleasant occupation, it has become an absolute necessity ; we are the sons of him to whom it was said after the Fall, " In the sweat of thy face thou shalt eat bread." " If any man will not work, neither let him eat."

In the same way unless we cultivate the talents we have received from God, we shall remain in low ignorance; we shall not develop the latent powers of our mind ; we shall indulge in monstrous vices without remorse. The Holy Spirit says in the Scripture, " I passed by the field of the slothful man : it was all filled with nettles, and thorns had covered the face thereof, and the stone wall was broken down." Laziness teaches many vices and brings on many miseries. We often see young peo-

ple without education who are good, excellent people, but it is because they are not idlers; they work
hard by day and by night. There is a glory in
work. But there never was an idler free from vice;
immorality, drunkenness, thievery often go hand
in hand with the idle man. Work is the shield of
virtue.

We have often seen pictures of the Holy Family,
but each one is depicted as busy at something.
Mary is represented as spinning, Joseph is at his
work-bench, Jesus is doing some minor thing ; but
all are at work. The scene is varied only when
they are represented in prayer. Go to that school
of labor, my dear children, there to learn application to your work. This must be your motto, at
study or in the workshop: work with Jesus before
your eyes. If you write, you may, with the eye
of faith, see your guardian angel bending over you
witnessing the movements of the pen. At your
age Jesus worked to the best of His ability ; you,
also, should do the same. Your divine Companion
was a laborer for the purpose of setting you an
example. When you grow tired, or rather when
you feel an attack of laziness, say to yourself :
" This work is for the glory of my dear Infant
Jesus. It must not be done carelessly, for then
it would not be worthy to be offered to Him."

Try to acquire a liking for work, by forcing yourself to it at first ; do not play when it is time for work ; encourage yourself by looking at Jesus at work, and a love of work will soon come. The obligation to work is in fact a religious obligation. We ought to work because we have to help others; if not now, at least in the future. It also conduces to health to employ the body at the work to which you are called. No work is low or unworthy of your dignity.

If you are a young man, still at your studies, thank Jesus that He has given you an occupation easier and pleasanter than was His. Then the assiduity with which He labored should spur you on to make such progress as your teachers expect of you. Our Lord, according to the Gospel, had little time to be taught ; but we have one example of His which will teach us how to behave in school. When He was twelve years old Our Lord remained in Jerusalem listening to the doctors of the law. He maintained there a grave silence; He was attentive and modest, and His manner excited the interest of the doctors ; they conceived such a great respect for Him that they did not hesitate to answer His questions and even listened to Him explain the Scriptures in His superior way. Keep, then, this picture before you of Jesus going to school : it is the only authentic one known.

· We read of the Blessed Virgin that in her childhood she served in the Temple. There the day was divided between study, work, and prayer. She used the needle in making things necessary for the house of God ; she studied the Scriptures ; she prayed as no one ever prayed before. You would gain many great graces if you placed yourself under her direction and invoked her help in your studies.

St. Thomas Aquinas, a Doctor of the Church and one of the most glorious teachers of our holy faith, studied and prayed. When he did not understand his studies he received enlightenment in his prayers. Often when he groped in the dark in his studies he wrote out his lesson, and placing the paper in his bosom he went to Mass, and then it somehow became perfectly clear to him.

Now, little worker, have courage in your undertaking ; the God who gave you this work will bless you, and all will become easy. Be not of the army of lazy people ; do not give yourself over to careless reading, or lose your time reading bad books. That is not work, at most it is a pastime. The life of man is but a day ; you are now in your youth, at the dawn of the day ; do not hesitate in the work that is before you, so that when the day is over you may say with Jesus dying on the cross, " It is consummated." Happy are you when you can say, " I have done my duty, and I have done it according to the graces given me." Christ will turn to you with a smile of content on His face as you leave this world of toil, and He will introduce you to the eternal enjoyment of rest in heaven.

The Mortification of the Child Jesus.

WE have to carry our cross to the end of our life ; no one is without a cross ; this world is so full of crosses that not only has each one his own, but there are a multitude to spare, so that if you escape one there are many others waiting for you. But these crosses are good for us ; they are the ladder by which we shall mount to heaven. Our dear Lord, the Child Jesus, offers to you also, my children, a cross : it is the cross of penance and mortification. This cross is necessary for our salvation, for it is the sign of it. It is the sign of the Christian who enters into this world ; this is a life which we enter with tears, because it is a sinful life. It is a short one, full of pains, miseries, and troubles ; a life of sickness and suffering in body, soul, and heart : such is life, and such has it been made by sin.

To accept all these inconveniences and contrarieties in a spirit of resignation and joy is already quite a great deal in the way of mortification, and we are bearing our cross which we received on en-

tering the world. But we know that this is not
sufficient. We must take on ourselves voluntary
penances which will give us strength to triumph
over our passions. We should be very much encouraged in doing this, for we know that the youth
of Christ was passed in mortification and privation.
Remember, first, that He was poor, He had nothing on this earth. See Him at table ; how was
He clothed, in what kind of house did He live ?
He lived among poor people, without luxuries,
sometimes without even the necessaries of life.

A holy Doctor says that sometimes, after a hard
day's work, Joseph could not get his honestly
earned wages and was forced, perhaps, to beg his
food. If Our Lord had but wished it, all that was
wanting would be forthcoming. But the Holy
Family wished to suffer the pinches of poverty in
order that you may learn to take sometimes of that
hard medicine of penance. We should not certainly be too dainty in our demands at table.

The Gospel tells us nothing of the secret sacrifices which the Youth Jesus had to make, nor
does it speak of the voluntary mortifications which
He added to His laborious life. St. John the Baptist in his youth lived a very holy and mortified
life. He was very young when he left his parents'
house to go into the desert ; he clothed himself

in a camel's-hair gown, he lived on locusts and wild honey, slept in a cave, and never drank any wine. He suffered cold, was exposed to the rain, the wind, the heat of the sun, on the edge of the desert near the banks of the river Jordan. Jesus saw His servant do this and commended him for it, and we may surely conclude that the youth of Jesus was passed in the same manner in Nazareth. Our Lord was so satisfied with the austere life of St. John the Baptist that He commended him publicly and received Baptism at his hands.

Fasts, retirement, mortifications of any kind, are not to the taste of worldly young men ; they despise them and are afraid of them, as if beyond their strength. Parents, too, become alarmed when they see signs of piety in their young men, as if holy practices would be detrimental to the health of their children. But the grace of God has always raised youthful saints who imitated the mortified youth of Jesus Christ.

Let us take at haphazard one example which is perhaps new. In 1832 there was in France a certain Sister Mary Rose who died in the odor of sanctity. From her childhood she practised astonishing acts of mortification. At the age of fourteen, with the consent of her parents and her confessor, she retired to a solitary place where she found a cave. There she lived on herbs, berries, and roots. " What more does a person want, when she loves God ? " she used to say. For seven years she lived there in prayer, work, and penance. Sometimes she went to the church to receive the sacraments, but these were the only times she left her abode. She then became a Sister of Notre Dame, and this was at a time when it was dangerous to have any religion at all in France. She was afterwards sent to the isle of Majorca, where she lived and continued her penances, and there she died a holy death. Many miracles were wrought at her tomb, so that at the present time they are preparing in Rome for her solemn beatification.

St. Basil and St. Gregory lived together in retirement in a pagan town, imitating in His honor the mortified life of Christ in Nazareth. During all the years that they resided in Athens for study they so mortified their curiosity that they never went out sight-seeing in that beautiful city ; they never went to the temples or the theatres ; they knew only the way to the church or to their school. What are we to think of those young people who are never happy unless they are away from home, free from the supervision of their parents ? Such people are enemies of the good Jesus who for thirty years hid Himself closely in a small, insignificant village, and never lost sight of His heavenly Father.

Jesus is not to be found in the busy bustling streets, nor in public gardens, nor in theatres where so many young people lose their innocence. Jesus kept a close guard over His eyes, He shut His ears to the scandals of the little world about Him, He watched over all His senses. How do we know this ? We know it from the actions of the saints, who, after all, were but a faint reflection of the beauty of the virtues of the life of Jesus. St. Aloysius Gonzaga was so modest with his eyes that his companions did not know the color of them. He never looked into the face of the queen whose page he was, though he met her often during the day.

Our Lord certainly did not listen to the grand music of the world : His character precluded such levity. He delighted only in the singing of the Psalms of David as rendered with greatest solemnity in the Temple. Worldly music we can avoid; it will not do much towards your education, nor add to your refinement.

Have the courage of your convictions as regards gambling : that is a vice which leads many a young man to destruction. When you feel you have a little money in your pocket do not choose for companions those who will show you gambling places where you can lose your money pleasantly, among alluring surroundings, in eating, drinking, and carousing.

St. Edmund learned from his mother, from his earliest youth, little acts of mortification. His mother taught him to fast on bread and water every Friday, and made for him a little hair-shirt, which he wore constantly. When he went to Paris to complete his studies his mother always sent with the linen which he needed some new, simple instrument of penance. "These are," she wrote to him, "the arms of a young man who is anxious to please his Master, Jesus Christ, and by them the purity of the soul as well as of the body will be guarded." St. Aloysius Gonzaga made for himself a discipline with which he scourged himself to the blood. He ate so little that it was true to say of him he was always fasting.

These little mortifications are agreeable to Our Lord, your model.

The people of the world look very sorrowful when Our Lord offers them His cross and tells them it is necessary to embrace it if they wish to go to heaven. They must, at least in their heart, despise many of the practices of the world which, if indulged in, make salvation very doubtful.

We certainly are not called upon to do great and extraordinary penances; still we ought not on that account think we need not practise any. There are many ways of mortifying ourselves which we will scarcely feel and which will not do us any injury. For example, we should not complain of what is placed before us at table; let us give up some favorite dish; do not eat or drink between meals, give up foolish or dangerous reading; rise a little earlier in the morning, and do so promptly; and many other little practices. Surely the divine Youth will consider us His friends if we do these things, and thus after bearing our cross in this life we may look forward to a crown in heaven.

The Charity of the Child Jesus.

WHEN we love God sincerely we must do what He commands. One of the great commandments of God is to love our neighbor : to love every human being, for every one is our neighbor, rich and poor, learned and ignorant, sick and well. The Youth Jesus whom we are considering in this little book had so much love for His heavenly Father that He could truthfully say, " I seek not My own will, but the will of Him that sent Me." God the Father committed to Jesus the office of saving mankind, and sent Him to this earth to fulfil that charitable mission. The youthful Saviour has already begun that work ; He had begun it in fact when He was conceived. A great service was done for the human race when He became man, just like ourselves in everything except sin. A young prince who, to make himself popular with his people, dresses like them, works as hard as they, and enters into their joys and sorrows, would be considered as giving positive proof of his condescension and of his love. Jesus in His youth and His child-

hood has done more than this.   He took upon
Himself the state and condition of a laborer, and
before preaching charity He passed His youth in
retirement, He labored hard so as to make our
lot the easier and to render more meritorious the
labors we do in His honor.   Charity is the sign by
which Our Lord recognizes His friends and His
disciples. This He has declared openly. Pagans and
Jews never practised the rule which desires us to
do unto others as we would they should do unto
us.   They held that revenge is permissible provided it does not exceed justice.   They thought
that all is done that can be expected when they
are kind to their friends.   But Our Lord coming
into this world taught a higher law of charity, a
charity so great that the most enlightened people
could not understand it.   He taught us to love
others as we love ourselves.   Jesus even went further : He loved us even more than Himself, since
He died for us to give us life, and to give us back
the right to heaven which we had lost ; He taught
that heaven would be closed on us unless we could
show that our love for our neighbor was perfect.

You must then love your fellow-men for the
love of Jesus ; all these are your brothers, and
Our Lord will reward you for the least service done
to them.   Do not vent your bad humor on your

companions, do not call them names, do not fight
with them and be spiteful towards them. Your
unkindness will displease the youthful Jesus, and
He will punish you for it, because you are not act-
ing as His disciple. So the charity of the good
Christian is not circumscribed by the narrow limits
of relations or acquaintances—it goes out wherever
it is needed. The Catholic youth will learn to give
alms, to relieve the poor, and to do good with the
money he can spare. Do not save your money in
order to spend it in a bad way, as many young
people do who see in money only a means of pro-
curing pleasure. They would rather gamble than
give to a good purpose the money risked at play ;
they would rather buy drink or tobacco with it
than relieve the necessities of others. A great deal
can be done by little savings though they be only
pennies ; but these pennies put together make
a very serviceable sum for a good purpose.

Give a little to the Peter's Pence, to the Society
for the Propagation of the Faith, to the Holy Infancy, to the support of a church. You can, if
really pious and full of faith, give towards the
ornamenting of the altar, or supply oil for the
lamp of the Blessed Sacrament. You may have
Masses said for the souls in purgatory, and occasion will offer to do many little kindnesses to your

companions, to the sick and the poor, even though
it cost you some of the money set apart for pleasure. Such holy, generous charity is very pleasing
to almighty God and to the Youth Jesus and they
have shown their approbation of it, so as to encourage it. Thus, St. John of God once found a
poor beggar lying in the street and unable to pro-
ceed further. The saint made himself acquainted
with the case, and finding that terrible sores were
on the beggar's feet, he procured what was necessary to put them in as good condition as possible.
Then, to see whether the sufferer was somewhat
relieved, our saint looked into the beggar's face,
when he was struck with the likeness it bore to the
face of Jesus Christ.

The young person who imitates the holy youth
of Jesus Christ will also be charitable in his words.
He will never speak evil of his neighbor, nor ca-
lumniate him. If you cannot speak well of a person, say nothing ; do not recount scandals or sus-
pect evil ; do not put a false construction on any
action. We will not see anything good in others
if we are continually criticising them.

Always give good example to others : as a good
Christian youth you are bound to do this on all
occasions and under all circumstances. In the
opinion of good people those who never have any-

thing good to say of their neighbor must be bad
themselves. Never to see any good in others, and
to lie about them, is about the worst reputation a
man can acquire. What a beautiful life our divine
Youth Jesus Christ must have led ! He never did
any wrong, and people saw this. He Himself has
said : " So let your light shine before men that
they may see your good works and glorify your
Father who is in heaven." The youthful Jesus in
conversation never blamed others or spoke of their
wrong-doings. Had He done so, how terrible it
would have been to the sinner, who knew that
Jesus read his heart !

Every day the Youth Jesus carried water to His
Mother Mary from the only well that even now is
found in Nazareth. Often the inhabitants asked
Him for some of the water He carried ; Our Lord
readily gave it, giving at the same time the same
grace which He gave to the woman of Samaria, the
grace of conversion. There is a tradition that one
day Our Lord had to go seven times to the fountain
before He could fetch water to His Mother. Great
must have been the charity of Our Lord ; the love
that was within Him continually showed itself for
others.

Just as Our Lord loved every one, so also young
Christians must love their neighbor and do good

to him. Do you also show such kindness to your neighbor ? Do you relieve his misery in every way possible to you ? God will remember every act of charity, and reward even a cup of cold water given in His name to the least, the most degraded fellow-man.

St. Martin of Tours, when still a catechumen,—that is, one who is preparing for Baptism,—and whilst he was a soldier, one day met in midwinter a poor man who had on scarcely any clothes. Martin cut his cloak in two and in the name of Christ gave part to the poor man. Jesus saw the action from heaven, for the next day Martin saw Our Lord wearing that piece of cloak and calling with exultation, " With this vesture did Martin the catechumen cover Me."

What a beautiful world this would be if all were charitable! There is enough good material in it to make a paradise of it. But perfect charity is too much wanting ; in fact each individual seriously fails especially in this one respect, that he has too little charity and feeling for others.

If in your youth you practise charity, what great things will you do when you have grown old in the service of your neighbor ! Nothing makes a man so great among his fellow-men as the spending of himself entirely in the service of his neighbor.

We may see the monuments of great statesmen, of kings, of inventors, but the greatest monument of all is the grateful remembrance of a charitable man.

When our day is over God will be kind to us and show us charity. After the judgment of the world, when all things are set to rights for eternity, you will hear the grand invitation : " Come ye blessed of My Father, possess you the kingdom prepared for you from the foundation of the world. For I was hungry, and you gave Me to eat ; I was thirsty, and you gave Me to drink ; I was naked, and you covered Me ; I was in prison, and you came to Me. Enter thou into the joy of the Lord ! "

The Zeal of the Child Jesus.

MY dear children, let us also imitate our dear Lord in His zeal. Do not suppose you have no reason to be zealous for God and His holy religion. Zeal is love of our neighbor put in practice : zeal makes apostles and enables them to bring many to heaven. Zeal is a burning fire which inflames our heart to make noble sacrifices. We, too, must have zeal because we have to contribute to the salvation of others. Jesus is the Saviour of mankind ; it is His privilege, His mission to save mankind from hell. Jesus means Saviour ; to save us He came from heaven ; for this He became man ; for this He established His Church. Every moment of the life of Our Lord was given over to that end to save mankind. His prayers and mortifications, His preaching, all His actions were destined for that end, the salvation of mankind. Our Lord, therefore, had a zeal for the salvation of souls ; it was His great delight to bring souls to God. Even before His birth He worked for the salvation of mankind.

It was He that influenced Mary to hasten across the mountains to visit St. Elizabeth, in order that St. John might be sanctified and that the precursor of Christ should not remain long in sin. As soon as He was born He **sent** out to gather in the good shepherds and bring them to the foot of the manger in order to fill their hearts with joy for the birth of the Messias. The zeal of Our Lord appeared in the childhood of Our Lord when the idols fell down and were broken in His flight to Egypt. He prayed that those people sitting in the darkness of idolatry might be converted. His prayer was heard, for those deserts were afterwards peopled by numbers of saints who lived there a pious, mortified, retired life. As Our Lord grew up His zeal also increased, the prayers, the tears of Our Lord were redoubled. What untold good was exerted on the young people about Him by His holy conversation and His good example !

You, too, my children, according to your ability and according to your age, must have zeal. Help Our Lord in the work He did, or, rather, continue the good work of zeal in which He was engaged. You are called to do something in this way, and you can do it at all times by good example : good example goes further, generally, than long speeches. The Latin proverb says that examples draw, whilst words will only move. When the young people of Nazareth saw the piety, the obedience, the industry, the sweetness of disposition of Our Lord, they wished to be like Him, they imitated Him, and practised the same virtues.

The fellow-students of St. John Berchmans were influenced in the same manner by his holy life; many became better for it, their hearts were raised to God, their conversation became chaste; so that we see that the blessed influence of the saint came upon those even who were unwilling to be led.

During the long time of Our Lord's retirement in Nazareth He saved souls especially by prayer. How much may you, my dear children, also gain by your prayers! St. Francis Xavier converted many thousand idolaters by prayer. St. Teresa once had a vision in which she was bid to pray and was told at the same time that her prayers were as fruitful in conversions as were the labors of the Apostle of the Indies. Pray, then, for the conversion of sinners, for the preservation in grace of the just, but pray constantly.

Many children belong to the Apostleship of Prayer, to the League of the Sacred Heart. This is a pious army which by prayer will obtain many graces from God. It gives you motives for prayer:

all the good works that may be done, all the necessities of the Church and of society, are suggested that you may make an effort towards doing good to all. A young man zealous for the love of God can invent many ways of approaching others to their good ; do some good, and you will find an opportunity of saying a kind word ; and, so, in a spirit of friendship you will recall others to their duty, you will induce them to pray, and lead them to go to confession and communion. St. Stanislaus had recourse to tears to atone for the offences done to God by his companions. He fainted when God's name was irreverently spoken or when improper talk was introduced ; so that his father would say, " Now, gentlemen, stop that talk ; you see what annoyance it gives to my beloved Stanislaus."

Zeal goes even to the prison where our dear dead are held in durance preparatory to being admitted to heaven ; by prayer, alms, fasting, communions, indulgences you can aid them. These practices of piety take the place of the flames of purgatory in cleansing. John Berchmans once found a small sum of money, which he took to a priest to have a Mass said for the souls in purgatory. But zeal reaches its perfection when at the call of God you renounce the world and consecrate yourself to the service of God in a religious house or by studying for the priesthood. What a great privilege it is to be God's servant approaching so closely to the throne of mercy ! Then you are a real apostle, you are called by a vocation peculiarly your own, you hear the interior voice and you hearken to it. You are proud of that calling ; you fit yourself from your school-days for college and the seminary. What an honor is such a vocation and what a blessing for a family ! It is the greatest distinction that can be given to a family to have a son consecrated to the priesthood. Do not mind your youth ; youth is the time to make generous sacrifices and to feel them least. Our Lord showed His parents that He had a right if He wished to use it, of leaving them and their protection. St. John was doing it ; why should not Christ ? When, therefore, Our Lord at twelve years of age remained in Jerusalem unknown to His parents and caused them great alarm by His disappearance, He wished to show parents that in the matter of vocation they must not interfere, but must allow their children perfect liberty, and help them, afterwards, in their honest choice. The vocation of youth is a most sacred right : what they feel within of a call from God must be respected by the parents. Of course the parents ought to be consulted, and with their advice and that of a pru-

dent confessor, there is generally no difficulty in
arriving at a happy conclusion.

In whatever career you find yourself be united
to the will of God and your zeal for the work as-
signed to you will prove your love for God.   To
all of us has been committed the care of the salvation of our neighbor, and we ought not say with
Cain's brazen effrontery, "Am I my brother's
keeper?"   At your daily avocation, at your studies, you may be your brother's keeper by giving
good example and counsel.   To save others is to
save yourself.   But pray to the Blessed Virgin
and to St. Joseph that they who looked after the
temporal welfare of the youth Jesus may also extend their care to you in this life and bring you
to a happy eternity.

And now, my dear children, let us ever bear in
mind the holy example of the Divine Child; let
our life be pure and innocent as that of the children He loved so well, and, following in His foot-
steps, we shall at last come to that heavenly home
which He has promised to all who become as little
ones.